THE BIG SWITCH

A BRIAN KANE MYSTERY

JACK BLUDIS

To Ponky
Pat
old friends
are the
best
always
Jack Blic

DESIGN IMAGE

THE DESIGNIMAGE GROUP, INC.

Copyright ©2001 Jack Bludis

The Design Image Group, Inc.
PO Box 2325
Darien, Illinois 60561
www.designimagegroup.com

ISBN: 1-891946-10-2

First Edition

THE DESIGNIMAGE GROUP, INC.

Printed In The U.S.A.

10 9 8 7 6 5 4 3 2 1

For Sosie, Ollie, Debbie and Linda,
women who made a difference.
And for my sons, Jay and Trev.

CHAPTER 1

With a hey, and a ho, and a hey noni no, I thought, as Noni Light pulled a coin from her sequined purse and clicked it to the surface of the counter at Schwab's Drug Store.

Schwab's was where Lana Turner was supposedly discovered by a talent scout for Warner Brothers. Even in 1951, every starlet in waiting wanted to be seen there. Noni was already a starlet at Morgan Studios, but she wanted something bigger.

She looked in my direction for a moment. Then she raised her nose and stepped outside. She was sexy in a Jean Harlow kind of way, with her hair bleached almost white and her lips full and red. It was a look I liked with Harlow, and one I liked even more now.

I left a dollar on the counter, which covered my breakfast and gave the waitress a hell-of-a-nice tip. I'd been following Noni for a week, but in the last twelve hours, she got to know me by sight, and I was losing my value. My two weeks on the case was almost up, and I knew a lot more about her and Lester Randolph than when I started. I knew about some other people too.

Noni was in Max Morgan's stable of starlets, the ones who played hatcheck girls and filled in the background for restaurant and bar scenes. They were also on call to do favors for studio executives and visiting dignitaries. As far as I knew, Noni never had a speaking role, but she was in a lot of crowd scenes.

Last night, she was on the arm of Roger Francene, one of the biggest stars in Hollywood. She spent the night at his house after a party there, but I didn't think there was any hanky-panky – at least not with Roger. Everyone in town knew, but the rest of the world would be shocked to learn that this he-man and hero had a preference for young men rather than women. Yet, Noni left his house at eight that morning, and a cab dropped her off at Schwab's.

I stepped into the sun and squinted as I hooked my very dark glasses over my ears.

Still wearing the same white dress she wore to last night's Morgan premier of *Madame Cruseau*, Noni strolled down Sunset, twirling her purse like a hooker in a bad movie. Before she reached the corner, she turned, put her hands on her hips, and shook her head violently. "What the hell are you following me for?"

"Me?" I said. Incredulity hardly ever worked, but it was worth a try.

"Yeah, you." She snarled and her face flushed. "As far as I know, I ain't messing around with nobody's husband, and I ain't stole nothing, so what's all this following me crap?"

"I don't know what you're talking about."

"You been following me since yesterday, and I don't like it."

I'd been following her and Lester Randolph for two weeks, but I wouldn't tell her that. "You're a good looking lady."

"Don't hand me that!"

When I didn't respond, she looked over her shoulder like she thought somebody else might be listening. Then she did a little toss of her hair, beckoning me toward her.

"Let's go someplace and talk about it." She had softened

her otherwise high-pitched voice.

"Sure." I didn't know what would come of it, but it was worth a shot.

She squinted with one eye and surprised me by suggesting her own apartment, which was just a few blocks away.

The buildings in her complex were long and low in California adobe. She mustered me past the huge bald man at the front desk and led me to her apartment. It was small, with one bedroom, a kitchenette and a living room, but it was far from cheap. French doors overlooked a pool, where a couple of copies of Noni as well as some assorted redheads and brunettes were lying on chaise lounges catching the golden rays of the Southern California sun. Apparently, nobody explained that at this hour of the morning, the sun was about as useful as flashlight for a tan.

Noni told me that all she had was Cutty Sark and Jack Daniels. I learned about Scotch in England. Now, even six years after the war, Scotch was still my drink, so I settled on the Cutty with water. In the kitchenette, she had a hell of a time crunching the ice cubes from the aluminum tray, so I helped her. Mostly what we got was flakes and chips instead of cubes.

"What's this all about?" she said.

I didn't answer as she fixed me a low-ball glass with Cutty and water over fragmented ice. She handed it to me, made her own drink of straight Jack over ice and carried it into the living room. It was early for a little girl like her to be drinking, but it was early for a big guy like me too.

I stepped over to the French doors and tasted my Scotch while I stared out at the starlets who decorated the pool. I especially liked the ones who untied the strings of their bikinis to avoid lines across their tans.

"Hey, I'm over here," Noni said.

I turned from the view to see her flopped on the couch, her legs crossed very nicely. She showed both knees and half-a-thigh. Almost bare legs in a movie aren't nearly as interesting as a leg with the strap of a garter belt showing through a slit a woman's dress.

"Why don't you tell me all about Lester Randolph?"

Her cheeks went cherry red – an inappropriate shade for Noni. She took a deep breath and a quick swallow of her Jack.

"Lester Randolph?" she said, raising her eyebrows, as if she had never heard of him. Incredulity didn't work for her either.

"The guy you meet on Tuesday and Thursday afternoons."

"I don't . . ."

She looked straight at me, her baby blue eyes showing beautifully against the blood-shot background of too much alcohol and not enough sleep. She showed guilt, confusion and fear, and with her chin raised, she thought she did a great job of hiding it all.

She grabbed her purse, unsnapped it and fumbled for a pack of Chesterfield's. I flicked open my Zippo and it was flaming before she even started her search for matches. She inhaled off my light and let out a long string of smoke, hoping I had a second question so she wouldn't have to deal with the first.

I had a lot of questions, but some of them, I wouldn't ask until she loosened up. I lit up my own Camel, slipped the Zippo into the side pocket of my seersucker jacket, and waited.

She picked a bit of tobacco from her tongue and rubbed her fingers and thumb over the stainless steel pelican beaks of her ashtray. The tobacco fell onto the reflective steel. Then she looked up. "Who hired you?"

"Who do you think hired me?"

"What is this, Twenty Questions? I just wanna know if it's

his wife or . . ."

I waited, but she didn't come through with another name. "I thought you told me you weren't messing around with married men?"

She didn't reply.

"You know California law?" I said.

"What d'ya mean?"

"We got something out here called community property. It means that everything a husband or wife owns gets split right down the middle in the event of a divorce, and divorce is a real possibility here."

"I don't know what you're talking about."

"He only gets to keep half. And the law also says he has to support the kids until they're twenty-one. The way he's playing around, it could cost him a hell of a lot more than half."

Her eyes widened. "What do you mean 'playing around?' Is there somebody else?"

She didn't want to know, so I didn't tell her. I was still wondering about "his wife or . . ."

"Just you," I said, but I was lying. For Lester, Noni was Tuesdays and Thursdays. On Mondays and Wednesdays, he had Gloria Hastings, a star at Regal Studios. For weekends on his boat, he had Lydia Lane, another Morgan starlet. I knew about Lydia, but I only just crossed her path with Lester. I hadn't really followed her.

Noni slumped and tasted her drink. "His wife's a real bitch, you know."

I didn't reply. Charlotte Randolph was a woman in her late thirties, beautiful and in good enough shape that I wouldn't kick her out of bed. I liked her looks a lot better than the skinny types that had been in style the last couple of years. She didn't farm her kids out to fancy schools like a lot of Hollywood people, but that was all I knew about her — except that she was paying me very well.

"She ain't gonna give him a divorce," Noni said. "She likes all the parties and stuff. It gets her picture in the movie magazines even if she ain't a star."

"Sure," I said.

I held my Camel between my finger and thumb like somebody sucking a reefer. That seemed to hypnotize her as she raised her low-ball glass and tasted the Jack.

After a few seconds, she squinted and tilted her head. "Are you sure it ain't Toby Wentworth who hired you?"

It was the name I was waiting for. He was also at Roger Francene's party.

"Why would Wentworth want you followed?"

Her cheeks flushed again. "I . . . I don't know."

Wentworth was a creepy little guy who came over from MGM to produce Morgan musicals. Unlike Roger Francene, he had an avowed letch for gorgeous women, especially women who could dance. At this point, I didn't know if Noni fell into that category, but she certainly had the body and legs for it.

"It ain't what you think," she said, and she took a quick sip of her drink.

"What do I think?"

I tasted my Cutty and waited. She was real slow on her answers, so I took a drag on my Camel.

When the silence became unbearable, she spoke. "I've never been to bed with him," she said, looking into her glass.

"So why would he want you followed?"

"You don't know anything about him, do you?"

"What should I know?"

"He won't hire a girl with any . . . scandal. He was almost involved with that moral's crap before the war. He's thinking of me for a speaking part, maybe even a singing part."

Sure, I thought, and if that didn't work out, he'd let her

direct his next picture.

"Please don't tell him about me and Lester."

I hadn't planned on telling him, but this didn't jibe with what I knew. Creepy or not Toby Wentworth had settled at least two out-of-court paternity suits. The movie magazines reported all his fine parties, but there were rumors that he had a lot of other parties that would sink anybody's contract on the morals clause. Noni had already lied to me once and there was no reason to think she wouldn't lie again.

"So you're totally faithful to Lester?"

"Yes." She raised her chin and held her cigarette at her ear in a Bette Davis pose, which didn't look right on her.

It was clear she now thought Lester was my client, and she was trying to convince me there was nothing between her and Toby. Noni might be a starlet, but she had no talent for acting, which was true even of a lot of people whose names appeared regularly on the marquee.

I drained my Cutty and set it on the cocktail table beside the twin-pelican ashtray. I took my Camel from one of the beaks, inhaled and snuffed it out.

"Why'd he hire you?" she said, desperate for information.

"Why did *who* hire me?"

"You told me it was Lester?"

"I didn't tell you anything."

"Oh, God. It *was* Toby."

I didn't answer.

"Please don't tell him," she said, leaning toward me and touching my arm. "I'll never get the part."

I felt sorry for her. She was like a lot of girls who came to Hollywood looking for stardom. She thought her face and body were enough, but out here, beautiful faces and luscious bodies are two for a nickel. She was just one of the crowd, as dispensable as last night's newspaper. It didn't make any difference if it were Toby or Lester or anybody else in Hollywood. They'd be nice to her as long as they got what they wanted, and she could play all the hat check girls and crowd scenes they gave her, but nobody would ever make her a star. They'd just use her until she was all used up. Then they'd dump her for the next beautiful kid from Waukegan, and Noni would be on the streets.

"Are you going to tell?"

"Tell who?" I said, rising from the chair.

"Toby."

She sighed and put out her cigarette. Then she rose slowly and looked up at me with her baby blue eyes. She placed her cool hand on my cheek and brought her face close to mine.

"If you don't tell him, we can –"

If she weren't so defenseless, I'd love to take her for an hour or two. All I had to do was lie to her or tell a misleading truth, and she would do every little trick I ever wanted from a woman and maybe some I hadn't even thought about yet. But too many people had lied to her already, and I wasn't going to join the crowd.

"I can make you feel good," she whispered, slipping her fingers inside my coat. Then she snapped her hand away from the bulge of the .38. She remade her smile and touched my chest inside the other lapel with the flat of her fingers.

"You're a beautiful girl, Noni, and you're still a nice girl. You got a chance for a good life, so why don't you go back to wherever you came from before it's too late?"

Her eyes filled with tears.

"I have to be a star."

"Good luck."

I would have smiled, but I knew it would come out sad or even sarcastic, and I didn't want her to see that. She was selling herself at any price to anyone she thought could help satisfy her dreams. The worse thing about it was that even Noni was beginning to realize that her dreams had already become nightmares.

CHAPTER 2

Charlotte Randolph said she wanted my report as soon as possible after she used up the two-week retainer, so I went back to my office and finished typing it up on my pre-war Underwood.

She said Lester spent every weekday at the studio, so I carried the report to the front door of her Beverly Hills hacienda. They hadn't got around to putting a wall around their house like some of the neighbors, but they had put an ornamental iron gate across the vestibule.

I waited, expecting a uniformed butler or a short-skirted maid. Instead, the inside door popped opened and a sleepy Charlotte Randolph looked out at me, her breasts pressing out against the gray silk material of her robe.

"Yeah?"

She stayed well behind the metal grate and squinted as if she had never seen me before. I tried to keep my eyes up, but her nipples kept jabbing at the silk and drawing my attention.

"I'm Brian Kane."

"That supposed to mean something?"

"I'm working for you – remember?"

"The hell you are!"

I leaned back as if she'd spit in my face. "You hired me

to follow –"

Wait a second! I thought. The face was similar but not exact. The cheekbones were high like the woman who came to my office, but this one wore very little makeup, and she was at least ten pounds lighter than the other.

"Aren't you Charlotte Randolph?"

"And who are you?"

"There must be some kind of mistake."

"You bet your ass it is. What do you want?"

"Didn't you stop by my office about two weeks ago?"

"For what?"

I took the envelope out of my pocket and held it toward her. "You asked me to –" I started to tell her, but I caught myself. This was *not* the woman who came to my office.

"Do you have a sister?"

"That crap again?"

"What crap?"

"There's somebody around this town who likes posing as me, and I'd damn sure like to find out who it is." She tilted her head, contemplating my value, maybe even my existence, but she nodded. "Come on in."

She yanked the chain that unlocked the grate, and led me into the house that was like a bit of Old Mexico.

I slipped the envelope inside my jacket and watched her walk as I followed her from the stone entry hall. She led me into the huge living room, with heavy Spanish furniture that had a lot of dark wood and even darker leather.

"Can I get you a drink?"

"No thanks. I already had an eye opener."

She sat on the leather sofa and crossed her legs. I expected her knee and thigh to pop out like Noni's, but she disappointed me.

"Now who's this woman who's been posing as me?" Her

voice, like the impostor's, was throaty. And, strangely, her diction was less refined.

"She's not your sister, huh?"

"No sisters. And who the hell are you?"

I explained that I was a private investigator hired by a woman claiming to be her. "She gave me a very nice, two-week advance," I said.

"And what was you supposed to do for her?"

I thought about the possibility that she was unaware of her husband's extra-marital habits and a rival might be using me to spring the news on her. After I weighed that thought, I realized it was not only possible but probable.

"I can't tell you that?" I said.

If whoever hired me ever bothered to show up, I'd give them the information they paid for, but I hadn't been paid to squeal on Charlotte Randolph's husband. What I did for a living was verify things people already suspected and find out very specific things people wanted to know. If she suspected anything, she didn't show it. She was more worried about the imposter.

"You're telling me that some bitch is running around Los Angeles pretending to be me, and I ain't got a right to know what she's up to?"

It would be easy to tell her, but I rose to my feet, deciding to keep my fee and get the hell out of there.

"Where're you going?"

"Since you're not the lady who hired me . . ."

"Wait a minute," she said. "What if I pay for that envelope you've got inside your jacket?"

"Why would you do that?"

"Curiosity."

"I don't work that way."

"What do you mean you don't work that way?"

"You're not the one who hired me."

Her eyes narrowed. Like me, she was good at weighing the art of the possible, and she sized me up pretty well.

"I'll show you out," she said with a snarl.

❖

I was in my office for about twenty minutes when my phone rang, and I stiffened at the voice on the other end of the line. "This is Mrs. Randolph. Do you have that report?"

I'd talked to them both now, and that was enough to know which was which. This was the one with the boarding school diction, the one who hired me.

"Yeah. I got it."

"Would you mail it to me, please?"

"Where?"

She gave the Beverly Hills address of the Randolphs.

"Can't do it."

There was a pause. "I paid for the report, and I want it mailed."

"If you want a report, you come and get it – or give me another address."

"What's the meaning of this?"

"I think you know."

Again there was a pause. Finally, she asked where my apartment was, and I decided not to argue. "I don't want to come to your office again."

I live in old Hollywood in a building that's not much better than a flop house, but it's a big as I can afford. I clean the place myself, and I pay my own plumber and electrician. My estate-sale furniture is a little too nice for the neighborhood, but it's comfortable. I gave her directions.

"I'll be there at nine," she said.

Actually, I had plans to spend the whole night with Kitty Chaney, my old friend and bunk mate, but I wanted to get another look at this woman.

"Fine," I said.

Kitty Chaney and I sat in the Brown Derby on Wilshire. Eduardo was strolling though and strumming his guitar, while I slashed through my prime rib and Kitty forked through her cobb salad.

"So you're telling me I have to go home by myself because you've got some woman coming to visit?"

"A client."

"Sure."

Kitty was tall and slim, with flowing dark hair and huge dark eyes, and she had the carved cheekbones of the department store model she was. She was also a high-priced call girl with a select clientele that included some of the biggest stars in Hollywood.

"You still got time to pick up a fare," I said, with more than a hint of sarcasm.

"I'll call my service and see if there are any messages," she huffed. Then she rose quickly and left the table.

Kitty made a decent living as a model, but she had expensive tastes, so her extra profession worked out well for her. We slept together a lot, but not always. It was stupid of me to make a date for nine o'clock when I already had one with Kitty at seven, but it might be my last chance to find out who was trying to pass herself off as Charlotte Randolph.

Kitty came back to the table, gorgeous and freshly made up. She might have hidden the fact that she had been crying from someone else, but I knew her too well.

"No calls. Are you sure you can't get out of it?"

"How about if I come to your place afterwards? I should be finished by ten."

She lived in a very nice, two-bedroom house on the fringes of Beverly Hills. I'd been there a few times, but that was a while ago. She said she didn't like company at home, and she never entertained there. "You know nobody ever comes to my place."

"Come to my place, then."

"Maybe I should meet you on a street corner."

For about five minutes neither Eduardo's guitar nor the conversation at the other tables penetrated the chilled silence, and the clicking of our knives and forks only accented our lack of conversation. Finally, I broke in with a play-by-play of what happened with Noni Light and the real Mrs. Randolph.

"Did you make love to her?"

"Who?"

"Noni Light."

"She's just a kid, for God's sake."

"That's never stopped you before?"

"She's a nice girl."

"That's never stopped you either."

"I told Noni to go back where she came from. I told her Hollywood would strangle her."

She tilted her head on her long neck and squinted. Finally she decided that she wanted to believe me, and she looked at me sadly. "You know if I didn't have this need for . . . God for everything, I –"

"Yeah," I said. We never talked about marriage, never talked about love, hardly even talked about liking each other, but I thought about all those things, and I knew she did too.

She reached across the table, covering my hand with hers. Trim and magnificent, Kitty looked even more beautiful with tears. She had a soul like no woman I had ever known, but she needed love and lots of it, and no one man could ever satisfy her completely. Not even a man *she* loved.

"I want to get to the bottom of this thing," I said.

"I understand."

What she knew but didn't understand was that I had a problem similar to hers. I liked lots of women. It was probably why we got along so well. It would be a hell of a lot easier if she could just accept that, but I didn't fully accept her problem either, so we just did what we did and made it work as best we could.

We had taken Kitty's M.G., one of those low, squared-off British things, and she dropped me off at the corner near my apartment and made me walk.

It was her way of saying, "Go to hell."

CHAPTER 3

I wasn't in my apartment twenty minutes when the other Charlotte Randolph came to my door, wearing a big hat, a veil and long navy blue gloves. On the white blouse underneath her navy jacket, she wore a sailor's tie. The outfit was a little too high fashion for me, I thought, as I gestured to the Louis the Something-or-other love seat in my tiny living room.

"I'd rather stand," she said, and when I turned to face her, she had a snub-nose .38 pointed at my chest.

"You're the boss," I said.

She filled her blouse and jacket more fully than the real Charlotte might, and she was taller.

"Stay right there and don't move," she said.

"I'm not going anyplace."

She tilted her head and squinted. "What's this business about not mailing the report?"

"What's this business about you not being Charlotte Randolph?"

She hesitated a moment, surprised that I picked that up, but she recovered enough to act tough again. "I'm the one asking the questions. You've got five hundred dollars of my money, and I don't like the run-around you're giving me."

"So sue me."

"Look, you son of a bitch, I could pull this trigger just as easily as –" She took a breath "Why wouldn't you mail it?"

"Because you're trying to break up somebody's marriage. If it were your own marriage, fine, but you've got no right to mess around with somebody else's."

"You rotten bastard," she muttered. She wasn't angry enough to pull the trigger, and she couldn't slap me without me taking the gun from her.

"Who the hell are you?" I said.

I saw her biting into her lipstick even through the veil. She was feeling sorry for herself, and she didn't realize I was moving closer. Her finger relaxed on the trigger, and the barrel of the snub-nose was slopping toward my knees. I didn't like the angle, and I made the first step fine, but the second was one too many and much too fast. She regained control of the snub-nose and brought the angle back at my chest.

I raised both hands. "Sorry."

"What did you learn?"

"Noni Light was seeing Lester Randolph and Toby Wentworth. Roger Francene was helping with the cover up."

"Who else was Lester seeing besides Noni?"

"Another starlet, a girl by the name of Lydia Lane."

"Who else?"

"And Gloria Hastings."

"That's what I get for a five hundred dollars?"

"Isn't three enough?"

She was thinking, and the gun relaxed in her hand again. This time she stared straight through my body to a point someplace on the floor behind me. With a quick grab, I had the gun out of her hand, and it took her a few seconds to realize what happened.

"You took my gun," she said.

"Look, Lady, what the hell is this?"

She looked up at me and laughed with a touch of hysteria. "Why are you playing Charlotte Randolph?"

"Her husband's running around on her. She deserves to know."

"Why?"

"Because I want him."

"And who the hell are you?"

"I'm her sis —"

"She doesn't have a sister."

Her face went to pain. "I'm nobody."

"But you have a name?"

"Nobody," she said. She was staring through me again. Finally, she looked into my face. "If you won't mail it, can I have it?"

I thought for a moment. I couldn't afford to pay back the five hundred dollars, and she did hire me to follow Lester. I'd give her the report — I just wouldn't deliver it to Charlotte for her.

"You paid for it," I said, and I slipped the envelope from inside my jacket. She fingered it open and read the four pages: two for the week I followed Lester and two for the week I followed Noni.

"Thank you. May I have my gun?"

I shook my head. "You're liable to hurt somebody."

She opened the door and turned to face me. "Thank you very much for the report." She hesitated for just an instant, then quickly left my apartment.

I put the snub-nose in my night-table drawer and called Kitty, but she didn't answer. I toggled the cradle and gave the operator the number of her service. I left a message that I would be home alone for the rest of the night.

But she didn't call.

I was still thinking about Kitty the next morning, when I found Detective Sergeant Kansas Michaels parked outside my office on Sunset. He was sitting in the front seat of his unmarked Ford, the wide brim of his hat down over his eyes. The stub of a cigar was clamped between his teeth, and his hands were behind his head.

I tapped the driver's side window, and he jumped.

"What the hell you doing scarin' me?" he said.

"I wasn't scaring you. I was waking you up. What do you want?"

"I'm comin' up."

It wasn't the first time he'd greeted me by sleeping in his car outside my office. It usually meant he wanted information. Sometimes, it meant I was in trouble – but not often.

He limped up the narrow stairs to the second-floor corridor, and I unlocked my office for him. As usual, he went straight for the chair behind the secretary's desk, pulled open a side drawer and propped his bad leg on it, his right leg. It had been a long time since I had a secretary, and I had a tendency to use this office more than the one inside.

Kansas and I were friends since the war. He was the son of a cowboy known as "Kansas Mike" who came to California to be in the movies, and played in grade-B Westerns until he died. Kansas the cop was never called "Junior" and Kansas the cowboy was never known by the last name "Michaels." Kansas the cop left home at sixteen and joined the army, intending to make a career out of it. He was a buck sergeant when he mounted a machine gun at Pearl Harbor and shot down a couple of Zeros. He was sent back to California with a Bronze Star and a right leg that had been gouged with shrapnel.

As an early veteran of World War II, he was accepted into

the Los Angeles Police Department, gimpy leg and all. His hair was thin through the middle and almost nonexistent at the pate, but I'm sure he didn't think of himself as bald.

"You get yourself laid last night?" he said.

"Nope."

"That's a shame." Kansas was thinking hard, which could mean trouble. "You know a cute little blonde, goes by the name of Noni Light?"

"Yeah."

He pulled the cigar stub from between his teeth. "Seen her lately?"

"Yesterday. Why?"

"Somebody bumped her off."

I took a deep breath. "Damn! A beautiful thing like that."

She was a nice kid no matter how many guys she was screwing. She just thought that was the way to become a star. I found myself wondering if the other Mrs. Randolph had anything to do with it.

"What are you all teary eyed about?" said Kansas.

"Your damn cigar smoke."

He looked at the ash and made a face. "Not lit."

"Smoke hangs over everything."

"Yeah," he said, and he looked at me with cold curiosity. It wasn't the way a friend was supposed to look at you.

"Tell me about Noni Light," he said.

"I had a drink with her, but that's all. She was alive when I left. It was ten in the a.m. on the nose. The job was up. You know I work by the clock."

"Yeah, you and that damn clock of yours. I never heard of a private dick who punches in and out like he's workin' in a defense plant."

He looked at me for a long time, waiting for me to comment, but he was out of luck.

"You'd never make a cop," he said. "Takes devotion."

"Sometimes I work by the job, sometimes I work by the hour. I'm in it for the money." But I was in it for a lot of things. Money was just part of it.

"Glad you told me about having a drink with her. She must've been killed early afternoon. Your finger prints might be around some."

"How'd she die?" I said.

".38 slug in the belly."

I though about the snub-nose I took from the Charlotte Randolph imposter.

"Where'd you go after you left her?"

"You don't suspect me, do you?"

"You been following her, right?"

I thought it was just a deduction, but he flipped open his pad. "We got a citizen's complaint that they seen some six-foot-one, dark-haired, blue-eyed Italian or Mexican looking guy following her in a gray '48 Ford for the last couple of days. What do you say to that?"

"Guilty. I was following her."

"Tell me about it."

I gave him a story that was the truth – with a few things left out. I didn't tell him that the Charlotte Randolph who hired me was not the one who lived with Lester Randolph in Beverly Hills, and I didn't tell him about taking the gun away from the impostor last night. What I held back could still embarrass me, but it was a chance I took. I didn't like the idea of somebody killing a beautiful young thing like Noni for no good reason, and I felt bad that I didn't see it coming.

"You sure you didn't kill her?"

"How long've you known me, Kansas?"

"Long time, but just for my peace of mind. Answer the question straight up."

"I didn't kill her."

He sighed and nodded. "You ain't planning on leaving town are you?"

"Come on!"

"You got Mrs. Randolph's address?"

"Sure," I said.

When Kansas left, I thought about calling the real Mrs. Randolph and asking her to cover for me, but she wasn't the kind of lady who would do a favor for a stranger. If whoever killed Noni Light was looking for a scapegoat, they had me to point to, especially if they didn't know I made a habit of taking care of myself. That might not help much if Kansas really suspected me of killing Noni. He was all business when it came to murder.

I waited around my office until I was sure he was out of the neighborhood. Then I went back to my apartment to take a look at the snub-nose .38 I took from the other Mrs. Randolph. I opened the drawer to my night table, and all I found was an almost full pack of Camels. The first thing that came to me was that when I took the gun away from the impostor, she was wearing gloves.

Now, the snub-nose was missing, and my prints were all over it.

CHAPTER 4

"STARLET MURDERED," screamed the headline. I dropped a nickel on the pile, picked up the top paper, and let the coins slide to the one underneath. I unfolded it and read the right hand column as I walked. The piece had an Andrea Anderson by-line:

> *Yesterday, Noni Light had her dreams of stardom*
> *ripped apart by a .38 caliber bullet in the stomach.*
> *The twenty-six-year-old starlet, featured in such films*
> *as* Adam Had 'Em *and* Ringside Table, *was murdered*
> *by someone she knew and trusted . . ."*

"Bull shit," I muttered, crumpling the paper like an accordion. I had half a thought to throw it away, but I unwrinkled it, folded it again, and carried it back to my office.

I smoothed it out on the secretary's desk and started to read.

It drove me crazy the way reporters like Andrea Anderson made assumptions that even cops couldn't make. They made things up, just to make a story sound more important, but the article told me a few things I didn't know. There were powder burns on the front of Noni's sequined dress, her apartment was in the name of the Morgan Studios, and she'd been "featured" in a couple of musicals. Featured players, to me, were those whose names appear before the picture starts. Andrea Anderson's definition, at least for the purpose of the front-page obituary, meant that Noni Light's face had appeared someplace on the screen as an extra.

Far down in the article she mentioned that an unnamed private investigator would be questioned about the case. That was me, and the questioning had already taken place this morning. There was another curious note at the very end of the article:

> *. . . Studio executives indicated that Noni Light was in*
> *line for an important role in the upcoming Morgan*
> *extravaganza* Jane, *a musical based on the exploits*
> *of cowgirl legend, Calamity Jane.* Jane *will be*
> *Toby Wentworth's first musical for Morgan.*
> *The Funeral will be held at the Chapel of the*
> *Psalms at nine tomorrow morning.*

I went over the Andrea Anderson article again to make sure I didn't miss anything. I checked the rest of the front page and the sports before I tore off page one and the narrow column on page three where the article concluded. I put them in a folder marked "Lester Randolph" and slipped the folder into my nonexistent secretary's middle drawer.

Noni Light, I thought, staring at the wall. She was a sweet kid. It was something you could tell, and I'm a sucker for the sweet kids. So many of them were destroyed when they finally realized that the prettiest girl in their school was just another face to the likes of a Max Morgan, a Louie Mayer, or any of a dozen other studio executives. If it wasn't for the way I felt about that, I might have gone to Kansas and told him everything I knew. It was his job to find the killer, but I wasn't satisfied.

I wanted to find out who killed her, yes.

But I also wanted to make sure they paid a price.

The phone rattled like a rusted bicycle bell. I looked at it for a few seconds and let it rattle a third time before I picked it up. "K.D.A.," I said.

It stood for "Kane Detective Agency."

"Kane?" Kitty said as if she were afraid to speak.

"Hi," I said.

"I got your message. I'm sorry."

"Sorry about what?"

"You know what. I didn't have to take a fare, but I thought you were going to be . . . Well, you know, all night."

"I know how you felt. I feel the same way myself sometimes. Why don't you come over to my place tonight? We'll have spaghetti and wine and . . ."

"Eight?"

"Eight's good," I said.

Kitty wrapped her arms around me the minute she walked through my door. She was still wearing one of the dresses she had modeled that afternoon, a low cut, straps-across, floral thing Carmen Miranda might wear if it had a train and she had a tropical-fruit headdress. Kitty kissed me long and lingering, but with the subtlety of a woman hungry for a gourmet meal.

"You're not mad?" she said.

"We understand each other," I said.

Her dark eyes searched mine. "Almost," she said.

Understanding was not the problem. Accepting was the problem.

She kissed me again. Then she took me by the hand and led me into the bedroom. We sat on the edge of the bed and kissed another time: lips, cheeks, ears, necks. We were like a couple of kids in the back seat of a convertible. I touched her left breast through her dress. After a while, I undid some of her buttons and gently lifted that same breast from her strapless bra. I touched the nipple with the tip of my tongue.

"Noooo," she cooed, as earnestly as a high school sophomore.

"Yesss," I hissed.

"Somebody's going to catch us," she said, experiencing the same fantasy.

"Let 'em," I said.

Slowly, we peeled each other out of our clothes. We touched and we kissed. Gentle touches, long kisses. What we had wasn't love, but it was something a hell of a lot like it, and it was nice. We made delicious love or sex or whatever you want to call it, and after a long while, Kitty was asleep.

I slipped into my boxer shorts and strolled to my closet-size kitchen, satisfied and happy. The water had boiled down and the spaghetti had burned to charred sticks, but the sauce was still simmering. I woke Kitty and we had Irish spaghetti sauce over Italian bread, with a Chianti chaser.

Noni Light's funeral was not the biggest in Hollywood history, but it was bigger than I expected. That was probably because more than the usual number of ordinary people who managed to get into the chapel with the stars.

Lester and Charlotte Randolph were there, sitting near the front. Lydia Lane, Lester's other starlet was with Toby Wentworth, John Huston was with Jean Hagen, and Clark Gable, who was still married to Sylvia Ashley, was with Marilyn somebody-or-other, the blonde who looked so good in *All About Eve*. Max Morgan was there, looking like the pompous ass he was. Louie Mayer was there with his wife, pretending he still ran MGM, when everybody knew Dore Schary was making all the big decisions. Andrea Anderson was with her six-foot-six photographer. Kansas stood alone at the back of the chapel, watching the whole show. When he saw me with Kitty, he nodded.

"A lot of big names for a girl who was a nobody," Kitty whispered.

"Publicity for the Calamity Jane Picture," I said, without moving my lips.

"What?" Kitty said.

She didn't understand. I'd tried to be a ventriloquist in high school, but I couldn't get the damn dummy's mouth moving in sync with what I was saying. I told her again about the Calamity Jane picture, and she said "Oh," but she didn't understand any better than the first time.

I stared through the non-celebrities, trying to pick somebody who was capable of doing an impersonation of Charlotte Randolph. I found two or three people who at first glance seemed like they might be right. But when I looked over at Mrs. Randolph to compare, they weren't even close.

After a while, I ignored the rest of the crowd and just stared at Mrs. Randolph. Her dress was simple and black. Her chin was raised with imperial carriage. I didn't remember her ever being in the movies, but she should have been. She had "star" written all over her.

Once I caught her looking over her shoulder and across the aisle in my direction, and she looked away, trying to put me in my place with a pretense of boredom. The chaplain was in the middle of the eulogy when I saw her standing in the rear of the chapel next to Kansas.

I listened for a moment longer as the chaplain praised Noni's "unfulfilled talents."

Sure, I thought. Then I did a double-take, to the rear of the chapel. The woman next to Kansas was gone. I looked front and saw that Charlotte Randolph was still in the second row with her husband. The one next to Kansas was the imposter.

I stepped quickly into the aisle and hurried to the back of the chapel. I walked on my toes, but there was still the scuff, scuff of my leather soles on the marble floor. A few people glanced at me, irritated. Kansas followed with his eyes, as I hurried past him and stepped outside.

I was blinded by the light, but I put on my sunglasses just quickly enough to see the other Mrs. Randolph step into a limousine. I hurried toward her, but the long black Cadillac pulled away. I tried to get the license number, but the limo moved too fast. It was already around the Wishing Well and on the way out of the cemetery when Kansas yelled after me.

"What the hell you doin'?" he shouted, as the limousine went through the gate and turned right onto Santa Monica Boulevard.

"That woman," I said.

"Yeah," Kansas said. "What about her?"

"She looks like Charlotte Randolph."

"So what?"

"She . . ." What was I going to tell him? That I lied to him, that the woman who hired me to follow Noni Light was not Charlotte Randolph at all but a look-alike who probably killed her. I didn't realize how out of breath I was until I laughed.

"You're nuts!" Kansas said.

I must be, I thought. I had handled the probable murder weapon, and I still hadn't explained to Kansas about the woman who was impersonating Mrs. Randolph. I was digging myself deeper into trouble, and if I didn't watch out, I might end up as the number one suspect in Noni's murder.

"Did you talk to Mrs. Randolph yet?" I said.

"Yeah. She tells me she hired you to see if her husband was running around on her."

I rocked my head to the side.

"She says you cleared her husband of any hanky-panky."

"Yeah," I said, but it was a non-committal "yeah" and not a verification.

Kansas looked at me for a moment as if he might question that, but either he decided against it or I had misinterpreted his look in the first place. For a moment, I was grateful that Charlotte Randolph had backed up my story. Then I realized she might only be protecting herself by trying to provide an alibi for her presence during the time of Noni Light's murder, as well as trying to establish that she had no motive or her own – unless somebody saw my report.

Kitty had to go back to the store for an afternoon show. I asked if she wanted to have dinner, but she said she was booked for the night. Business always overruled friendship – and whatever else it was we had.

I was in my office, deciding which bills to pay and hoping for someone to come in and offer me an interesting and lucrative job that would pay them all. When the phone rang, I thought it was my lucky day.

"Kane?" said a rough voice on the other end of the line.

"Yeah?"

"Stay out of Noni Light's business."

"Sure," I said, smiling at the forced, tough-guy sound on the other end of the line. "She's dead. What kind of business does she have now?"

"Smart ass."

"Who is this?"

"You don't want to know," said the voice and there was a click.

I wanted to know.

CHAPTER 5

Roger Francene answered the front door of his Palm Drive Mansion in stocking feet, a red silk robe, and disheveled hair. I wondered if anyone in Beverly Hills had servants anymore.

"What can I do for you?" he said.

His voice was soft, yet under the softness was an implied threat. It was just like in the movies, but here I could tell he was acting. That voice, the unkempt hair and the scar under his left eye were the marks of the characters he played.

On the screen, he was tall, which added to his image of ruggedness. He played cowboys and war heros, lovers and historical figures. In popularity contests, only Clark Gable beat him. Women swooned when they saw him on the street, but without his elevator shoes, he was half-a-head shorter than me.

"My name's Kane," I said, "I'm investigating the murder of Noni Light."

"Oh?" he said. Then he swallowed, realizing he might be in trouble. "Uh . . . come in."

His place was like an old English manor house, with a stone entryway and a balcony overlooking the front door. He led me to the living room where a huge fireplace stretched up the wall to the peak of the cathedral ceiling.

He motioned to one of two wine-colored sofas in front of

the fireplace that were separated by a huge, rectangular cocktail table. I sat on one of the sofas, and he sat on the other. Except for a spot that lit the conversation area, the place was dark. It must have belonged to Bela Lugosi at one time, because I'd swear there were bats in the rafters.

"How can I help you?" The threatening edge to his voice was gone. In its place was a crack of apprehension. He was treating me with the deference reserved for a cop or someone else in authority.

To keep it that way, I took out my old police pad and looked at my notes. "According to what I have here, Noni Light spent her last night alive in your house."

"I see," he said, trying to recover that tough-guy voice, but he wasn't able to pull it off. "Yes . . . uh . . . I had a party. There were a lot of people here. Yes . . . Noni was among the guests."

"And what time did she leave?" I said dryly, doing my impersonation of a police detective.

"Oh, I don't know . . . uh . . ." He sucked in his breath and looked up at me. He didn't know if I had facts or just suspicions. He thought for a moment and decided to play it straight – in a manner of speaking.

"Noni had a lot to drink," he said. Then he chuckled. "A lot of people did. I was her . . . uh . . . date." Again he chuckled. "We went to a premier. She . . . uh . . . fell asleep and . . ."

"Let's try this again: what time did she leave?"

He had a tough time saying it, but the words finally came. "Well, It was eight or nine in the morning when I sent her home in a cab."

I nodded. So far, so good. "How well did you know her?"

"Not terribly well. She was one of the up-and-comers on the Morgan lot. I just needed a date for the premier and, well, I . . . uh . . . guess she was convenient."

"What about last week?"

His ears tinged pink and rosy color bled through the tan of his cheeks.

"Pardon me?" he said.

"She stayed at your house last week too. Want to tell me about it?"

"Tell you . . . uh . . . Oh, I had a party then too. You know how it is with these good-looking girls. Everybody wants to be seen with them. As a matter of fact, I liked her very much."

"Why weren't you at her funeral?" I said, raising my eyebrows. The pink at his cheeks turned red.

"I mean, I didn't have a thing with her. Not love or anything. We slept together some, but . . ."

What he was telling me was not necessarily true, but it was what he thought I wanted to hear. He was watching for my reaction. He was getting nothing, and it was making him uncomfortable.

"How long have you been seeing her?" I said.

"Six months maybe?"

"Every Monday night?"

He looked curious now. "How did you know?"

"I know a lot of things," I said.

He squinted and tilted his head. "How did you know that? Did she leave a diary?"

I smiled. "You want to give me the details?"

"She was very good in bed," he said, smiling at the corner of his mouth.

Now, he was acting, going back to the he-man he portrayed on the screen, but he was carrying it into parody, and he reminded me of that guy Sid Caesar on Saturday night Television.

"How many times did you go to bed with her?" I said,

I grinned, letting him know I doubted the lie he wanted to

tell. I waited and he sighed.

"This isn't coming out right, is it?"

I just looked at him.

"You don't think I killed her?"

I still looked.

He sighed and looked up into the rafters. He tapped all ten fingers together as if he were deciding whether to pray. If those millions of women who loved his on-screen image could see him now, they would push all thoughts of him out of their beds. On screen, his image was solid. Here, it was breaking down to the reality of who and what he really was.

"Are you accusing me of killing her?" he said.

I shook my head.

"Then what do you want?"

"Who was she seeing?" I said.

"Just me," he insisted.

I shook my head again.

He was about to betray a trust, and he didn't like it. Finally, he sighed again and crossed his arms. He looked at the cushion on the sofa beside him, uncrossed his arms with a flourish and waved both hands at me.

"I know I'll get into trouble for this, but I'll get into more trouble if I don't tell you." He sighed and crossed his arms again. Then he continued. "She was seeing Toby Wentworth here at my place and . . . Lester Randolph, sometimes."

"Both at your place?"

"Of course not. I don't think they know about each other. Noni was very good at keeping secrets." Now, even some of the depth of his voice had slipped away.

"Did she love either one of them?"

"Lester. I think she loved Lester, but I'm not sure. I do know that she hung all over Toby, but I think it was because she wanted to be in one of his pictures."

"*Jane*?" I said.

"Yes. The one about Calamity Jane. How did you know about that?"

I just looked at him, not mentioning that I read it in Andrea Anderson's article.

"Of course," he said. "You're a policeman and . . . you know a lot of things. Well, she was going to play some dance-hall girl with a couple of speaking lines. At least Toby Wentworth told her she was, but I think he was telling the same thing to every starlet on the Morgan lot. Noni's chances were worst than anyone's."

"Why?"

He smiled sadly. "Poor Noni. She had no talent at all. None."

"She must have had some talent," I said.

He chuckled. "You mean in bed. Oh, yes. Yes, she was very good in bed. Very, very good. Almost as good as a man."

It was a casual acknowledgment that, although he preferred men, he was not adverse to making love to an occasional woman.

"Do you think Toby would want her dead just to keep her out of his movie?"

"Of course not. If you knew Toby, you would know he doesn't give a damn about anybody's feelings, and I mean anybody's. He said Ethel Merman might be a good musical comedy star, but she was not a movie star and he refused to have anything to do with *Annie Get Your Gun* as long as she was involved. He said it to her face! That's why Louie Mayer picked George Sidney to direct. As it turned out, Ethel was so steamed she wouldn't take the part, and they gave it to Betty Hutton. That was Toby's last straw with MGM. That's why he's with Max Morgan now."

He cackled and continued. "Toby wanted *Jane* to be

finished at the same time as *Annie Get Your Gun* so they could have some head and head competition, but Max Morgan said 'not a chance.' Toby could make *Jane* after *Annie Get Your Gun*, but not before, and it would definitely not be released at the same time. He said he didn't want to split the audience with Metro. He just wants to mop up and get all those biddies who can't get enough musicals. *Jane* is an original by some nobody screen writer and a contract composer. It's a whole lot cheaper to do that way than to deal with those Broadway people."

Roger rambled on for another five minutes about how the studio was different when old Sam Morgan was in charge, but none of it had to do with the death of Noni Light, at least not as far as I could figure.

"Where were you the morning she was killed?"

"Right here, I guess. I walked her to the door to get the cab. Then I went straight back to bed."

"Where was Wentworth?"

"Oh, he pulled the 'I gotta get home' routine and left about five o'clock, but I'll bet my last nickel he was off to some other tramp."

I didn't like the way he said that, and I glared. "Is that what you thought of Noni?"

"Not Noni. The others," he said, scared to death that he had made himself a suspect.

He was a suspect all right, but it wasn't because of any disparaging remarks he made about Noni. There was something strange about him other than the fact that he was not the he-man, nor even the man, the public thought him to be. I didn't quite know what it was, but it seemed awfully important.

"You're not doing any pictures on location are you?" I said.

"What do you mean?"

"You won't be leaving the Los Angeles area for a while, right?"

"Oh, no," he said. "Of course not. Oh God, no."

"Good. I might have some more questions for you," I said, and I let him lead me out of the mansion. He still thought I was a cop, and it was better that way.

Before he closed the heavy paneled door behind me, I turned for one last question. "Who was Noni seeing on Wednesdays?"

He looked at me confused.

"You were friends, weren't you?"

"She wasn't seeing anybody," he said, raising his nose.

That may or may not have been true. All I knew was that Lester Randolph was seeing Gloria Hastings, and Noni seemed to stay in her apartment on Wednesday nights, but there was more than one way in and out of her building.

I wondered why he answered the door without his elevator shoes, but I didn't ask.

In the morning I picked up the phone and gave the operator the number of police headquarters. When I got through to the switchboard, I had to wait for Kansas.

"Anything new on the Noni Light case?" I said, when I finally got him.

"What d'you want to know for?"

"You know me, Kansas. I was following the girl. She got herself killed. I don't like that."

"Who does?"

"Why are you so sour this morning?" I said, and I pushed the rolling chair back from the secretary's desk and propped my feet on the bottom drawer that was already pulled out.

"I had a bad night," Kansas screamed over the phone. "All right?"

"If you say so," I said.

"Wait a minute." Kansas went away from the phone. I lit up a Camel, and blew a few smoke rings while I waited. I hoped he wouldn't come back with the news that he found the murder weapon and that my prints were all over it.

He didn't.

"You know a starlet by the name of Lydia Lane," he said.

"Yeah?"

"Why do they always have the same letter on both names?"

"Is that what you wanted to ask?"

"No, you smart ass. When's the last time you seen her?"

I thought for a moment. She was on Lester Randolph's boat Sunday and at Roger Francene's party after the premier.

"At Noni Light's funeral," I said. "She was with Toby Wentworth."

"She's the one, huh?"

"Yeah," I said. I moved the phone from one ear to the other. "Why? Did something happen to her too?"

"Not as far as I know. We just wanted to ask her some questions."

I thought of telling him about her weekends on Lester Randolph's boat, but I was already in trouble for knowing too much. I'd be in more trouble when he or one of his people interviewed Roger Francene and learned that I had been there first.

"What else?" I said. There was a fleck of something sticky on the mouthpiece of the phone and I scraped it away with the nail of my index finger.

"You writing a script?" Kansas said.

"Everybody out here's writing a script. I want to find out who killed Noni."

"Sometimes you make me nervous, Kane. You know that?"

"I make everybody nervous – sometimes."

"Why do I get the feeling that you know something I don't?"

"Because I always know more than you do," I said, laughing, and I took a drag on my Camel.

"If you got something to do with this, you better let me know before I find out on my own."

"I don't know anything," I said, "but if I get something, I'll call you. I saw what the papers said, but I need some stuff from you."

"You want to play twenty questions or do you just want information?"

"Give me the thumbnail."

Kansas, on the other end of the line, bounced his phone to the desk, jolting my eardrum. In a few minutes, I could hear him shuffling papers. Finally, he spoke.

"Blonde, female caucasian. About five-five, hundred pounds. Goes by the name of Noni Light. Real name, Naomi Lichtenstein. Indianapolis, Indiana. Shot from about six inches, once in the stomach. Sperm deposits in last twenty-four hours. That wasn't you by any chance, was it?"

"No such luck." But almost, I thought. "Were there any foot prints? Prints in the carpet that could help? Mud? Shoe scuffs?"

"High heeled shoes. Probably hers."

"Find the weapon?"

"Nope, but ballistics says it was a .38."

"Thanks," I said, and I eased the phone to the cradle.

I made a mistake by calling him. Kansas is one of the smartest cops I've ever met. He already made an assumption that I knew something he didn't. Maybe not something as serious as my guess that my prints were on the gun, but once the weapon showed up, I'd have a lot of explaining to do.

I was sitting on my far-too-elegant, estate-sale love seat watching the Kraft Television Theatre and nursing a bottle of Sunshine State Beer when the phone rang. I picked it up, hoping it was Kitty telling me she cancelled a fare so she could be with me tonight. But it was luck of a different kind.

"Brian Kane?"

I registered the voice with my memory and decided it was the real Charlotte Randolph. "What can I do for you?"

"I been trying to get you all day. You the guy who wrote me this letter?"

"What letter?"

"This thing about my husband and Noni Light, and about Noni and some other people. This the crap you didn't have the guts to say to me in person?"

I asked her to read it. After only a few lines, I told her it was my report. "The woman who posed as you must've sent it."

"How much you want for it?"

"Me? Why would I want anything for it? It was bought and paid for."

"I said I'd pay you. You didn't have to throw it in my face like this."

"I didn't send that to you, Mrs. Randolph. I guess the lady I worked for did." Apparently she missed it the first time I told her.

"Oh?" There was a long pause. "I want to know some other things. Can you come over Saturday? I'll pay you."

"Won't Lester be home?"

"He goes out on his boat all weekend. He can't be bothered with the family."

I loved the throaty sound of her voice, and I loved how she looked in that gray robe. And I damn sure wouldn't mind seeing her again.

Besides, I needed every penny I could get.

"What time do you want me there?"

CHAPTER 6

I parked my three-year-old Ford along the long, white wall that completely enclosed Toby Wentworth's place. The gray of my car seemed dirty against all that white. The white wall was exactly what I'd expect from a director-choreographer, I thought as I hit the intercom button outside the pedestrian gate.

On a hill just twenty yards inside the wall stood the white, two-story house. It qualified as a mansion.

"Yes," said a very deep, very gruff male voice.

"My name's Kane. I'm investigating the murder of Noni Light. I'd like to speak to Mr. Wentworth."

"Just a minute," said the voice. It was too deep for Wentworth. At least somebody in Beverly Hills still had servants.

"Come in," said the voice through the intercom.

There was a buzz. Then I pushed open the pedestrian gate and made sure the lock clicked behind me. The walk to the house was all up hill. A man of about six-foot-eight with a long, ugly face opened one of the double doors. He looked out of uniform in the penguin formality of bow-tie and tails.

The floor of the huge entry hall was polished marble. Fred Astair and Ginger Rogers might come tapping down the wide, curved stairway any second, I thought as I followed the giant into the white carpeted living room. There was white furniture, white statues, and a white fireplace. The room he took me to was also white, with white chairs and a white carpet. Toby Wentworth was in a white suit behind a white desk.

By now, I was snow blind.

"Perfect place for a white sale," I said.

Wentworth gave a closed-lip smile, but he was not amused. On three of the walls were autographed photos of stars and posters from the dozens of movies Wentworth had choreographed and directed since he went independent from Buzby Berkeley in the thirties. The photos were in black and white. The wall behind him was all glass, a series of French doors overlooking the wide stairway that went down to the pool.

Wentworth motioned for me to sit, and I did.

"Terrible about the girl," he said.

"Yeah."

"Such a sweet girl, talented too." He shook his head and made a "tsk, tsk," sound. "Now, what can I do for you?"

He leaned both elbows on the desk and tapped his fingers lightly together. The change from anger to sorrow to business showed him to be an excellent actor as well as an experienced dancer, choreographer, and director.

Small and small-featured, Wentworth was more delicate than Roger Francene. Comparing the two men, most people would think that Toby rather than Roger was the homosexual, but in Hollywood, it was Toby Wentworth who was noted for his wild parties and his escapades with starlets. A rumor said that Toby and three women had been caught in bed together. They were high on marijuana. It was about the same time that Robert Mitchum and Lila Leeds got busted. They say Max Morgan used every bit of influence he had to get the Wentworth incident covered up.

I opened my pad. "I have information that you were at a

party at Roger Francene's house the night before Noni Light was murdered."

"Hmmm. As a matter of fact I was – but so were a lot of other people."

"I understand you stayed most of the night. And so did she."

He looked at me, trying to read my mind by studying my face, but he gave it up. I waited for him to speak.

"Roger was still there when I left," he said.

"And?"

"We're friends," he said, after a while.

"Then you know that Roger Francene isn't likely to spend a night with Noni Light or any other woman."

He raised an eyebrow and leaned far forward. "Sounds like you've been kicking around in the Hollywood rumor mill too much."

"Tell me where I'm wrong?" I said, wanting him to verify something Roger had indicated.

"Roger Francene's strange, but he's not . . . well, not totally strange. He likes *some* women the way men do."

He was waiting for me to acknowledge that I knew what he was talking about, but I just stayed quiet and looked dumb.

He continued. "What I'm trying to say is that he likes men and women."

"And he spent all night with Noni because he was in the mood for a woman that night?" I looked straight at him.

Finally, he leaned back and crossed his arms. "She was a talented kid."

"You already said that."

"I mean, she could sing, she could dance, she was beautiful..."

I believed the beautiful part. At least, she was almost beautiful. The rest, I didn't know about.

"She . . ."

"Why don't you make it easy on yourself?" I said.

Now, he studied me even more closely. He didn't know I wasn't a cop. If he had, he would have thrown me out. What he did think was that he was getting to be a suspect in Noni Light's murder, and he was weighing whether the truth or a lie was the best way to go.

"I slept with her . . . and Lydia Lane until about five, five-thirty maybe. Then I came home."

His response was juicier than I expected, but it did jibe with what Roger told me.

"How many times a week do you see them?" I said.

He flushed red and leaned back in his white chair. Very consciously, he was trying to determine how much truth to tell, knowing that either too much or too little could get him into trouble.

"Well . . . I've seen Noni about twice a week for the last couple of months – I missed a day last week though. I've seen Lydia a couple of times. It was my first time with both of them. Lydia didn't like it. Neither did Noni, but she faked it. She's, uh, she was very good at that. It was a shame she couldn't act except in bed."

So much for his lie about her being a talented kid. I asked him to tell me about the Calamity Jane picture, and he was surprised that I knew about it.

"Doesn't anybody read the papers?" I said. "Andrea Anderson had it in her front page story about the murder."

He sighed. "She thinks she knows everything, doesn't she? . . . Well, neither Noni nor Lydia is strong enough to be Jane, but I planned to cast one of them in a side bit as Belle Starr."

I thought back to the history of the Old West and tried to remember if Belle Starr and Calamity Jane ever knew each other. I didn't think so, but I guessed in the movies, it didn't matter.

"Did you get them together in bed for some kind of

a contest?"

"Of course not," he said. He was angry at first. Then he smiled, "But that's not a bad idea."

"Except that Lydia wins by default?"

"Unless I test her against someone else," he said, still smiling.

He was so pleased with himself that I wanted to punch out several of his too many teeth.

"Look, I haven't seen Lydia since the funeral," he said.

"Does Lydia know she has a chance for the part?"

"Not at all," he said. "But thanks for the suggestion about the test."

I nodded. It was strange, but this son of a bitch with his white house and white suit and his arrogant attitude seemed like exactly the kind of man who could take two women to bed and let them pretend they were satisfied.

The fact that Lydia thought she might be considered for a part in *Jane* forced me to add her to my list of suspects. But for all of his apparent truth-telling, it was Toby Wentworth who went to the top of the list.

"When were you planning to shoot the picture?"

"Three months," he said.

"Who's playing Calamity Jane?"

"That's not public yet."

"Can I know?"

He looked at me long and hard, deciding how much cooperation was absolutely necessary. Finally, he shook his head.

"I'm the only one who knows," he said. "And for business reasons, I'll keep it that way."

I looked back at him, snarling and nodding, but I wasn't able to shake him. He might or might not be a murderer, but he was definitely a shrewd businessman, and he was not going to take any chances on me blabbing to Andrea Anderson or anybody else.

"I understand," I said.

He seemed to bend over backwards to answer all my questions, but I detected that he wasn't telling me the whole truth. There was a lot about him I didn't like and even more I didn't trust. I told him I'd see him again in a few days.

I knew from following Lester Randolph that he made a habit of spending his weekends with various starlets on his yacht at the new marina they were beginning to cut out of the marshes behind Venice. He hardly ever went out on the Ocean and not at all since I had been following him. In the past, I was satisfied to let them sit there until Sunday night when I followed him home. This time, there was more to learn.

It was after dark when I parked my Ford on Pacific Avenue and walked back to the marina. Randolph's baby-blue Packard convertible was on the lot. The lights in the salon of the fifty-five foot cruiser were lit, but the shades were drawn.

I waited until a power cruiser cast a wake, rocking the boat, and I timed my jump to the rear deck so Randolph wouldn't sense anything out of order. I moved closer to the windows and sat against the bulkhead. The rumble of the cruiser was still audible and Teresa Brewer screeched out "Music! Music! Music!" from a radio inside the cabin.

After I keyed my attention, I heard somebody turning the pages of a magazine. I waited for a long while, and I was almost asleep when I heard Randolph say, "You want a drink?"

"Got one," said a voice I recognized as Lydia Lane's. I heard the clink of glasses and the sound of someone sloshing something over the ice and stirring a drink. It was a long time before they talked. I could hear my own breathing, but from experience I knew that no one inside could hear it.

"The police are looking for me," she said, casually.

"What?"

"I called for messages. The desk says it has something to do with Noni."

"What are you going to tell them?" Now, he was forcing himself to be casual, but I could hear him tinkling the ice nervously in his glass.

"Whatever they ask."

"About me?" he said.

"If they ask."

"That's not a very good idea, you know."

"Why?"

"It certainly won't help your career," he said.

"Is that a threat?"

"You know me better than that. It's just that if it gets back to Charlotte . . ."

"You and your precious Charlotte!" Lydia jumped up so hard from wherever she was sitting that she rocked the boat.

"Don't take that attitude," he said, softly.

"What attitude should I take?"

"You know how I feel about you."

"Sure," she snapped.

There was more movement, more rocking of the boat. Apparently both had jumped to their feet. In a moment, Lydia's breathing was hard. Then it was muffled. There was silence, probably a long kiss.

"How do you feel about me?" she whispered.

"You know."

"Yeah, I know," she said bitterly. "About the same way you felt about Noni."

"Noni's dead. Don't talk about her," he said, anger in his voice.

"Did you kill her? Is that why you don't want me to tell the cops about you?"

"Don't say that!"

"Why not? You didn't kill her, did you?"

"Of course not."

"Who was it then?"

"How the hell should I know?"

"How about that woman. The one who looks like your wife."

"Shut up about her," Randolph said.

"Is she trying to blackmail you again?"

"I knew I shouldn't have told you about her."

"She was, wasn't she?"

"Of course not. I haven't talked to her in months."

There was a long pause. Probably another embrace, another kiss.

"Who killed Noni?" she said, with a whimper.

He never replied, but the boat rocked as he apparently swept her into his arms, like in so many of his movies. He must have carried her down to the master cabin. I moved at about the same time they did and got a place outside the porthole where I could listen. All I heard were grunts, groans, and sighs.

I got no new information. All I got was horny.

I waited a long time. Then I heard snores.

It might not be a waste of time to stay, but if I ended up falling asleep, I'd get caught, and that didn't make any sense.

I went back to my apartment and called Kitty. When there was no answer, I called her answering service.

"She not expected to call back until tomorrow," the girl said.

Apparently, Kitty had a fare. I hated that, but that was Kitty and that was us.

CHAPTER 7

When I went to the grate covered vestibule of Charlotte Randolph's house Saturday morning, a boy of about eight opened the door and led me into the living room. He had brown hair, with dimples like his mother and blue eyes like his father, and he was wearing short pants and an adult-looking polo shirt.

"Won't you have a seat," he said, like a miniature adult.

He motioned to an upright Spanish chair with wooden arms and leather upholstery. Then, standing near the fireplace, he cocked his head to the side and studied me. It was the pose of a male model in Esquire. Maybe a pose he had seen his father use.

"Are you a policeman?" he said.

"Private Detective," I said, smiling.

His eyes widened. "Like Sam Spade and Phillip Marlowe on the radio?" he said.

"Something like that?"

"Wow!" he said. "I never met a real, private eye before. Do you know those other guys?"

"Only on the radio," I said.

"Oh," he said, disappointed.

I stood as Charlotte came into the room, her hair wet and

stringy. From the dark spots on her terry cloth robe, I knew she was wearing a wet bathing suit underneath.

"I wasn't thinkin' about the time," she said, and she vigorously rubbed a towel through her hair.

"He's a private eye, Mother. Like Sam Spade."

Charlotte raised her eyebrows, surprised that I had surrendered the information. Perhaps she was even a bit angry as she wrapped the towel around her head like a turban.

"Go watch your little sister for a couple of minutes," she grumbled. "I'll be right there."

"Yes, ma'am," said the boy. He looked confused for a moment. Then he pulled his polo shirt over his head and hurried away. What I thought were short pants turned out to be bathing trunks.

"He thought I was a cop. I had to clear it up."

"Yeah, sure. I hope he doesn't say anything to Lester. Sit down."

I did as I was told. "I want to thank you for covering for me," I said.

"What d'ya mean?" she said as she sat in a similar chair just a few feet from my knees.

"When Sergeant Michaels called on you, you could have told him you weren't the one who hired me, and I would've been in a hell of a lot of trouble."

She reached into the pocket of her robe and took out a crumpled gray envelope. I recognized the stationary from my office.

"Now, I *do* want to hire you," she said. Her chin was raised and her fingers were trembling as she held the envelope in my direction. It was my report to Charlotte the Imposter. "This says a lot of things I didn't know about my husband. I want pictures. I want a divorce."

"Don't you think you ought to talk to him about it first?"

"And put him on his guard? Not a chance. I've been taking care of him and his house since before the war. I thought he was something special. Now that I know all this stuff about him and these other women . . ." Her face turned sour and she shook her head.

He was a fool, I thought.

"And there's another thing I want you to do," she said. "I want you to find out who this bitch is who's trying to come off as me." When she spit the word "bitch," she stood up and slapped the envelope against her left hand. She glared at me for a moment.

Then the snarl disappeared and her eyes widened in horror.

I thought she was coming at me, and I leaned away from her, but she rushed right past me and into the dining room.

"My God!" she screamed as she banged through the French doors and onto the patio.

I hurried after her, wondering what the hell was going on. Then I saw a little girl of about four violently pedaling a toy racing car along the lip of the pool and at an angle toward the deep end. One front and one rear wheel came over the lip and the car hung for a long moment like an image in a slow-motion film.

Then it slipped off and into the water.

"Judy!" Charlotte screamed.

The little girl's screech stopped as her head went under the water.

"No!" the little boy shouted, and he ran toward the pool, but he was too late. The toy car was already in the water and on its way to the bottom.

I raced along the edge of the pool and dove in at an angle. My eyes opened as soon as I hit the water. The racing car seemed to glide downward, with the child trapped inside, her blonde hair flowing behind her. Bubbles poured from her mouth as she tried to continue her scream and I heard it. I cut through the water without a stroke. Even before the car hit the bottom, I had my hands around the child's chest. I peeled her free of the toy car, and the car sunk to the bottom of the pool.

I held her tight and tried to swim but my clothes were soaked and heavy, my shoes felt like lead weights. It was impossible to rise to the surface, so I lifted her over my head and walked along the bottom of the pool, and I hoped she was getting air. When I reached the wall, someone snatched her from my hands, and I grabbed the rungs of the ladder. I pulled myself hand over hand until I broke the surface of the water and flipped myself to the concrete. I lay face down on the painted surface, gasping for air.

"I'm sorry, Mother," the little boy cried. "I didn't see her."

The little girl alternately wailed and choked. It happened so fast that she didn't even have a chance to fill her lungs with water.

"It's all right, sweetheart. It's all right," Charlotte said to both of them.

I lay exhausted at pool side for a long while, as Charlotte told Judy she was all right and assured Jimmy he had done nothing wrong. I was trying to regain my breath, and I realized they were gone. After a while I slipped into something like sleep.

I don't know how long it was before a shadow came over me, blocking the warmth of the sun, but I let out a long breath and rolled over on my back. Charlotte stood over me with Judy in her arms. The child was wrapped in a towel and sucking on a lollypop. Jimmy stood next to them, holding onto his mother's robe, his thumb in his mouth. He was too big for that, I thought, but it wasn't my job to tell anybody.

"Thank you, Mr. Kane," Charlotte said.

"All in a days work," I said.

"A private eye and life guard too," Jimmy said, taking his thumb from his mouth. "That's really something."

"I'll get you some clothes," said Charlotte. "Take one of the bath houses." She motioned with her head toward the three adobe bath huts along the north side of the pool.

"I'll be back in a couple of minutes," she said.

I watched her hips swing through the robe as she took the kids to the house. When they were inside, I stood and looked down at my wet clothes. I must have looked like a bum.

The changing hut was nearly as big as my apartment. There was a large room with a sofa and a chair, another room with a bed and a dresser. There were wall hooks and hangers. I peeled out of my wet clothes and went into the full bathroom that included a tub with a shower. I was adjusting the shower when I heard a tapping at the bathroom door.

"Mr. Kane?" said Charlotte.

"Just leave the stuff out there. I'll get it."

"Open up," she said. "I got a towel."

I opened the door a crack and she reached in with a towel the size of a small bed sheet. Her hands were just beginning to show the wrinkles, but her nails were beautifully manicured. The way her fingers lingered, I had the feeling that if I just took her hand she would come inside with me, but I remembered that the kids were around someplace.

Even after I took the towel, she let her hand stay for a moment. Then she eased it away and closed the door. My chance was gone, maybe forever.

"What do you drink?" she said through the wood.

"Today? Scotch on the rocks."

"I'll get it," she said.

I thought about the way I had seen her just a few days ago in that gray silk robe. She was certainly the kind of woman with whom I'd liked to spend a few leisurely hours, but to suppress the thought, I let the shower run cold over me for a long time. Then I washed, stepped out, and wrapped myself in the huge towel.

In the bedroom, she had laid out a pair of white duck trousers, a red and white polo shirt like Jimmy's and a pair of canvas deck shoes. It was the outfit I should have worn to the marina, I thought. I felt like picking up the phone and calling someone just so I could say "old chap," and I grinned to myself.

There was a Scotch over rocks on the table next to the bed, and I tasted it. It was the good stuff. Maybe Johnny Walker Black.

When I stepped out into the sun, Charlotte lay stretched out on her stomach on one of the chaise lounges. She wore a fresh, white bikini, with the top strings untied like the girls around the pool at Noni's apartment hotel.

"How's Judy?" I asked.

Surprised, she went up on both elbows and her breasts swung free in front of her. Instead of covering herself immediately or getting angry at me for looking, she glanced at the front of the duck trousers and smiled.

"The kids're taking a nap," she said, holding the top of her bikini over her breasts and swinging her feet to the concrete.

"I wouldn't think a kid as old as Jimmy took naps," I said.

"He's probably fooling with his oil paints. Tie me up," she said. It was a leading line that I didn't take. She twisted her back to me, and I pulled the two strings together and tied a bow.

"Ooooo . . . your hands are cold!" she said.

"The glass was cold."

"Want another?"

"I'll take a rain check," I said.

In the reflection of the pool, I caught someone in an upstairs window. I looked in that direction, and Jimmy stared out at me.

"He's not sleeping," I said, nodding toward the house with my head.

"He doesn't have to be. Nothing's going to happen here."

"Where then?"

"Cocky, aren't you?" she said.

"Just wanted you to know how I feel."

"When the place is right and the time is right, maybe. What were we talking about?"

"The woman who's been . . ."

"That bitch's been hounding me. I don't think she lives in Hollywood. I think she comes and goes. I first heard of her about three years ago, when she tried to blackmail me and Lester."

She adjusted the chaise so her back was at a forty-five degree angle. Then she swung her feet up to the cushion and put on her big sun glasses. She laced her fingers behind her head and closed her eyes.

"Blackmailing you? How?"

"How else? Pictures. I never saw them but Lester says she looked a lot like me, only heavier."

"Old pictures maybe?"

"Don't be a smart ass. I ain't ever been any heavier than I am now."

"She was fat?" I said.

"'Plump,' Lester said. Not even real plump, 'just a little extra here and there,' he said."

"You didn't see the pictures?"

"He wouldn't let me."

"What happened?"

"He told them to get lost."

"Them?"

"Some guy," she said. "A chauffeur at the studio was the

one trying to put the bite on us. Instead of calling the cops, Lester got him fired."

"Was that the last you heard from him?"

"Him, yeah. Her? Every once in a while she shows up someplace. Time before now was about a year ago. She got an audition with John Huston, claimed to be me. She got the part."

I raised my eyebrows.

"John insisted it was me," she said. "I told him he made a mistake, but he says I should call him if I ever want to get in the movies. With John that means he wants to do more than just put me in a picture."

"Didn't he know about her?"

"He knew me. He didn't know her. She's that good an actress, I guess. Maybe I'll audition for him now that I know about Lester."

"And the kids?"

"Eh, you're right. I ain't givin' them to nobody."

I found out that Charlotte had been a child fill-in on the MGM lot, and she was in a few Republic Westerns during the war. I didn't remember seeing her on the screen, but I had no doubt she was good.

"You ever audition for Toby Wentworth?"

"Toby?" she laughed. Then she sat up straight and snapped her sunglasses from her face. "Toby hates Lester, so Toby hates me. He wouldn't give me a part unless he needed somebody to burn at the stake."

"Joan of Arc?"

"If he could really burn me."

I asked about the Calamity Jane picture, but she knew nothing more than was in the papers. Then I got back to the business of the imposter. "Why do you think she tried to pull it off this time?"

She shrugged. "Maybe she wanted to break up my marriage."

That was my theory. "If that's what she wanted, I guess she succeed."

Charlotte started to speak. Then she closed her mouth and looked down. There was a quick intake of breath. "I guess she did, huh?"

When she looked up, she was almost in tears.

Just a few seconds ago, I was ready to ask her about the right time and the right place for her and me, but I had already blown the opportunity. I shouldn't have spent so much time letting her get misty about her husband.

"I want you to find her," she said. "And I want you to get pictures of my husband and one of his bitches, and I don't care which one it is."

"The husband part will be easy. What good'll it do if I find *her*?"

"I'll claw her eyes out," she said.

That night, Kitty and I were carrying our shoes and strolling barefoot along the beach at Santa Monica. We didn't say much at dinner, and we said even less as we padded though the dry sand.

Kitty seemed to have something to tell me, and I was feeling guilty about my afternoon with Charlotte, even though I didn't do anything. Our fingers were hooked together as we walked, but our hearts weren't in it.

"We can't seem to get together anymore, can we?" Kitty said.

"We never can when I'm working," I said. I forced a smile, but she didn't look at my face.

"But you're doing it on your own time. Why?"

The quick answer was that I wanted to find out who killed Noni Light. It was also the real answer, but Kitty didn't want to hear that.

"I'm getting paid now," I said. Actually all I was getting paid for was to get photos of Lester and some woman. Any woman.

"Oh, yes. I forgot about Little Miss Homemaker of Beverly Hills, U.S.A."

"Don't make fun," I said. "It's good money. Besides, *you've* got two jobs."

"You're not funny either," she snapped.

"I'm sorry," I said. "I know how you feel about that. I shouldn't make jokes."

We trudged through the sand another five minutes or so.

"Do you think I ought to get help?" she said.

"What do you mean, 'get help'? Just because you like making love? Hell, everybody likes making love when they get used to it."

She stopped and looked up at me. "It hurts you, I know that, but it hurts me too. Drives me crazy. Should I see a shrink?"

Kitty not only liked sex, but she was a top-priced call girl and very selective of her clients. If she gave that up, what would it do to us? I had a need too: most of the time what I had for women was just sex, but it was also a need. If Kitty were "cured" and stopped seeing other men, what would it say about the way I handled other women? Would it mean that I had to be cured too? Or would it be the end of us?

"We've both got a problem," I said, "but I like you very much." I tried to hug her, but she froze and leaned away from me.

"You're not supposed to say that. You're never supposed to say that. Not 'I like you very much' and definitely not 'I love you.' That's not us," she said, and her eyes filled with tears reflecting red and green from the lights on the boardwalk. Suddenly, she struggled out of my arms and dashed across the beach.

"Kitty," I called after her, but she kept running.

Her sandals slipped from her fingers and when she stopped to get them, I grabbed her and wrestled her to the sand.

"I'll never say it again, I promise," I said. She was breathing hard, her eyes exploring my face.

"Make love to me as much as you want, as often as you want, but don't call it anything. Just do it and never give it a name."

"Yes," I said. "Right now. Right here."

"Yes," she said. "Here. Now."

She fumbled with my belt buckle as I pulled up on her cotton skirt and yanked down on her silk pants. I covered her lips with mine as she grabbed me and guided me to the place I wanted to be. She sucked air through her teeth at the very moment I entered her.

"Oh! Yes. Yes. Yes," she cried louder and louder and I hurried to catch up. Her screams subsided, and she started up again. After a while, we screamed together. As we sighed our endings, we heard applause from the boardwalk.

I started to laugh, and she started to giggle.

"Want to do it again?" she said.

"Not on stage," I said, my laugh subsiding. "Let's go to my place and we'll do it all day tomorrow."

"Yes, and maybe tomorrow night too."

CHAPTER 8

Sunday was terrific, but Sunday night Kitty was called to go to a party. She said she'd like to take me along, but the whole thing was part of one of her fares.

"I understand," I said, but I didn't.

As much as I try to understand, I still get jealous when I think of her with other men. I tried to figure it out Sunday night as I sat watching Ed Sullivan. Sometime before the show was over, I fell asleep. When the National Anthem came on, I woke up, took a shower, and went to bed. I wanted to call Kitty and talk to her just for the hell of it, but that would have been too much like checking up on her.

On Monday morning I went to my office and found the door unlocked. I pushed it open, expecting to see Kansas sitting behind the secretary's desk with one of his cigars clamped between his teeth. Instead, I found Lydia Lane, sound asleep on the fake leather sofa. She was curled in a fetal position, and the bare skin of her legs showed between her stockings and her white panties.

"Hey," I said.

She didn't move, but the second time I was louder, and I nudged her shoulder with my fingers. She jumped to her feet and looked straight into my face with bloodshot eyes.

"What is it?" she said, confused about where she was.

"It's me. Brian Kane," I said calmly. "You were asleep in my office. How'd you get in here?"

She looked around the paneled office frantically. Then she put the fingers of both hands to her temples, trying to connect the here and now with the there and then, but also trying to get away from a nightmare.

"Somebody's trying to kill me," she said, her brown eyes wide.

She moved closer to me, as if for comfort. Apparently, the here and now was as frightening as her nightmare.

I offered her a Camel, but she didn't smoke. While I zipped up one of my own, she eased herself to the edge of the leather sofa and tried to prove modesty by pulling her skirt as far over her knees as it would go.

"Who's after you?" I said, sitting on the edge of the secretary's desk with one foot touching the floor.

"It's . . . it's gotta be whoever killed Noni," she said.

"One of the other starlets?" It was a reasonable guess, but there was far too much involved for that to be the easy answer.

"No. Somebody real big. Lester Randolph maybe."

"Why would he want to kill you?" I said, remembering she had spent Friday night on Lester's boat.

I knew about her regular meetings with Lester of course, but I wanted to hear it from her. She told me a lot of things I already had before she came to something new.

"He thinks his wife is on to us," she said, "but he don't want a divorce. He says it'll be too expensive."

"So you figure because Noni's dead, he did it, and he wants both of you out of the way?" I shook my head. "That's not reasonable. He doesn't have to kill you, he just has to stop seeing you – unless you're planning to blackmail him?"

"Of course not," she said, and she was genuinely insulted. Lydia, like Noni, was one of those sweet kids who wouldn't think of blackmail in a million years unless someone they loved or feared put them up to it. But if that happened, she'd probably do it without a thought.

"When's the last time you saw him?"

She hesitated only a moment. Then she told the truth.

"Yesterday. On his boat."

"What did he do that scared you?"

"I made the mistake of telling him that I knew about him and Noni. He said he'd kill me if I ever told anybody about it. He told me to shut up about him and me too. I think he would kill me. I really do."

"How do you feel about him?"

She looked down at her fingers and played with a flake of nail polish. She peeled it off in a strip and rolled it in a little ball. Finally, she sighed and looked up.

"I love him," she said, her eyes glistening.

"So what makes you think he killed Noni?"

"Noni said she was going to tell Andrea Anderson about them. She said if she did that, she was sure to get the part of Calamity Jane."

"That doesn't make any sense."

"She said that if the world knew about her and a star, that would make *her* a star!"

It still didn't make any sense, but if Noni believed it, it would give Lester a reason to kill her. Maybe I didn't know Noni as well as I thought.

"What did *you* think?" I said.

Her cheeks flushed, and she looked down at the brown and beige linoleum tiles on my floor. "I kind of thought it was me who would get the part. Toby said I looked the part."

Toby would never give her the lead, and the whole thing was a stupidly honest admission for a girl who might be suspected of killing her friend. It made no difference that Toby Wentworth thought of her in a minor role. If Lydia thought she was in line for the lead, it was a motive any Hollywood jury would understand.

I didn't think she killed Noni, but a lot of things were starting to add up to wrong totals, and I wanted to get clear about them.

"How did you get my name?"

Her cheeks turned pink. She was stuck for a moment. Then a look of discovery went over her face.

"I found it in the yellow pages," she said.

"I'm not in the yellow pages."

"Yes you are. It's a teeny little ad."

I had tried to fake her out, but she had me on that one. Her description of the ad was perfect. My one line said, "Kane Detective Agency, Brian Kane, Investigations," and it gave my Sunset address and phone number.

Still, I didn't believe she looked me up. Somebody gave her my name and my number. I kept pushing, but she didn't tell me, nor would she admit she got me anyplace but the yellow pages.

Lester might send her to me, but he wouldn't tell her to accuse him of murder. Toby Wentworth was a more likely candidate, but I didn't believe that either.

"You want me to protect you from Lester?"

"From whoever is trying to kill me," she said. "Whoever killed Noni."

"Who do you think it is?"

She shook her head without looking at me. "I don't know. I just know that somebody wants to kill me, and I don't want to die. I just want to be a movie star."

Just like Noni, I thought. "Do you intend to see Lester again?" I said.

"Yes."

"Even though you think he wants to kill you?"

"It's probably not him," she said, but there was no confidence in the "probably." She wasn't sure about anything, and she was terrified.

"Who else could it be?"

"Anybody," she whimpered. "Everybody. Hollywood."

"That doesn't answer my question. Who else?"

"His wife? Roger Francene?"

"Why would you need protection from Roger?"

"I don't know," she whispered.

"Why?"

"I don't know," she said, and she looked up at me, pleading. "I don't know anything. All I know is that I need protection?"

"Night and day protection?" I said, raising my eyebrows.

"Of course not! I can't afford night and day protection. Besides . . ."

She looked at me, hurt in her eyes. It was the way I had raised my eyebrows. I didn't realize how lecherous it looked. I wouldn't mind spending a few days and nights with her, but I didn't mean to imply an invitation.

"So what is it you think I can do for you?"

"You can keep me alive," she said.

It was frustrating. Occasionally, somebody came to me to do bodyguard work, but clearly Lydia was not here to ask for that. She also wasn't asking for advice or self-defense training. As a matter of fact, she hardly knew why she was here herself.

"Who sent you?" I snuffed out my Camel in the ashtray and stood over her.

"I came here on my own. I'm scared."

"Of what?" I said.

"Of Lester. I know he's going to kill me." She bit into her lipstick and she jumped to her feet. Tears were starting to gather in her big brown eyes.

"How do you know?"

"I just know. I don't know what to do. I just heard you were special. You're supposed to be very good. You're nice. You don't take advantage."

"Where'd you hear all of this?"

"You know how to treat a lady."

She stepped closer to me.

"Where did you hear it?" I said.

"No place. I don't know." She couldn't look up at me, but she was beginning to weakly finger the lapels of my poplin jacket.

"Who? I'm not going to help you unless you tell me."

Her fingers pulled tighter on my lapels, and she pressed her forehead against my chest.

"Who?" I said.

"A girl named Kitty," she whimpered, and I went limp.

"Kitty?" I said. Why would Kitty recommend me to anybody? And what the hell did she think I could do?

"I met her at a party last night," she said.

My heart was pounding. I took her upper arms and held her away from me. I knew the kind of party Kitty sometimes went to, and I tried not to think about it when she left. I didn't want to imagine her and Lydia in bed with some guy, but the more I tried not to think about it, the more Kitty and Lydia and a vague "other man" came into my thoughts.

"When?" I said, trying to erase the pictures that were in my head.

"I told her I wouldn't tell you that —"

"When?" I insisted.

She looked up at me. "Last night. She told me last night

at Toby Wentworth's house."

Now, it wasn't just a guy. It was Toby Wentworth in an all white room on an all white bed in all white underwear with Kitty naked – and it made me sick.

"What's the matter?" she said, looking up at me.

"Nothing! How did you get in here?" I said. I had to get Kitty off my mind.

"The door was open."

"Bull shit!"

"I thought you opened at nine o'clock. I knocked and nobody answered. The door was open, so I came in."

I was still angry at Kitty, but there was something else now. Somebody got into my apartment to get the snub-nose .38 too, and Lydia didn't seem like the kind of kid who went around picking locks.

"Can you protect me?" she said.

"Why don't you just tell Lester that you're through with him and none of the story of your affair will ever get out, and –"

It suddenly occurred to me. I was now working for Charlotte Randolph, and my instructions had been to get pictures of him in bed with anybody. I might be cutting off a healthy fee. I was acting too much like a nice guy, and I wasn't a nice guy. I made my living by screwing up other people's lives.

"He'd really kill me if I tried to walk out on him. I know it."

"What the hell do you want me to do, lady?"

I was angry at Kitty and angry at Charlotte. I was angry at Lester and Toby. Most of all, I was angry at myself and I was taking it all out on Lydia. As her tears slid through her mascara, she looked like a sad clown, and I started to feel like a monster.

I pulled her into my arms and held her close. I didn't want to make love to her. I just wanted to comfort her, to make her feel just a little bit safer and maybe to be comforted a little myself.

"Can you help me?" she muffled into my chest.

"I'll try," I said, but I had no idea what I could do for her. If I spent every minute with her and somebody wanted to get her, they'd get her, and nothing I could do would stop it.

"It's probably your imagination," I said, but I didn't believe that.

CHAPTER 9

I found out that Lydia lived in the same, sprawling apartment hotel as Noni Light. The apartments were paid for by the Morgan studios so their starlets could live in semi-decent style while being paid virtually nothing.

In terms of an agreement, Lydia had no idea what she wanted me to do for her. I told her I'd keep an eye out for her, and check in with her periodically, and she was to let me know the minute somebody threatened her.

I refused to accept a fee but it wasn't charity on my part – far from it. I was planning to catch a photo of Lester Randolph with somebody. It might as well be her – I didn't want to be struggling with divided loyalties. Money was my first master, and the fee I was getting from Charlotte would cover my time and trouble, but that didn't keep me from worrying about Lydia. I didn't worry about Noni, but Noni didn't tell me she thought her life was in danger, and nobody was killed until her.

I spent most of my morning making notes on what I learned following Noni Light and trying to piece it together with what I found out since her murder. I called Kitty, but she wasn't at home. I called her modeling agency and asked where she might be working. They said she wasn't working today, and that bothered me. I wondered where she was, but I shouldn't even be thinking about that. Our understanding called for complete independence.

At about one, I got hungry and decided to go over to Jimmy's for one of his famous Hawaiian hamburgers. I stepped into the hazy brightness, hooked my sunglasses over my ears and started across Sunset. I waited in the middle of the street for a black limousine to pass, but it slowed to a stop and someone unwound the back window. I expected him to ask for directions.

"You Kane?" a man said gruffly from inside the limousine.

"Yeah?" I said.

"Get in," said the man.

It was the exact kind of demand I was likely to refuse under normal circumstances, but he had a .45 automatic focused on my nose.

"Who are you?" I said to the bore of the .45.

"Don't ask no questions. Get in."

The man who held the automatic was big and bald, and he spoke with the same tough-guy sound of Kansas Michaels, but this guy's sound was decidedly New York – and not by way of Uncle Sam like Kansas.

I know from my experience in the army that a .45 automatic is not very accurate over about five yards. But I also learned that up-close it can make a hell of a mess.

The way I figured it, I wouldn't get two yards before he pulled the trigger and I'd get a hole someplace in my back. He pushed open the door and slid slowly across the seat, making sure I didn't make a break for it. There was something in his tone that said he wanted to talk to me real bad.

I slid onto the beautifully upholstered leather and closed the door behind me. The bald guy had slid all the way to the other side of the car.

"Lock it," he said, and I did.

The guy in the front seat was young and good-looking. Like Noni and Lydia, he may have come to Hollywood to be a star. Maybe he got sidetracked, I thought, but he might also be just some guy from one of the mobs back east.

"To what do I owe this gracious invitation?" I said.

"You carrying heat?" said Baldy.

"Would you believe me if I told you I wasn't?"

"Reach inside your jacket with just your finger and thumb and pull it out by the grip."

"Who says it's inside my jacket?"

"Don't be smart. Just do what I say?"

I pulled the .38 out of my shoulder holster with my forefinger and thumb the way he had instructed and dropped it on the seat between us. Sometimes I'm stupid and sometimes I'm brave, usually at the same time, but this was not one of those times. The stupid part was getting into the limo in the first place, and now it was too late for bravery.

"Just ride around, Jeeves," said Baldy to the driver.

He didn't give it that phony inflection, so I assumed it was his real name.

"You got it," said Jeeves.

"How long you been workin' in this town?" said Baldy.

"Since the war," I said.

"And you been doin' a lot of fooling around with these Hollywood types, right?"

I nodded without taking my eyes from his, which were an evil brown, almost black.

"What do you say you stay out of this one?" Baldy said.

"What one?" I said.

"The Noni Light murder," he said, and I realized he was the one who threatened me on the phone.

"Why?" I said.

"Because I'm suggesting it."

"Why?" I said again.

"You're an inquisitive son of a bitch, ain't you?" he said.

"Very."

"You gonna keep being cute?" Baldy said.

He cocked the .45, and I felt as stupid as a snail. I had been so hypnotized by the open end of the automatic that I didn't even notice it wasn't ready to fire.

"Why do you want me out of this?" I said. "You got something to do with it?"

"Look, I ain't answering your questions, and I ain't gonna ask you any. I'm just tellin' ya to get off the case and let the cops handle it."

"They'll screw it up."

"I know," said Baldy. "That's why we want you out."

"Why don't we just kill the son of a bitch," said Jeeves.

"Boss wouldn't like that," said Baldy.

All along, I had the feeling Baldy was the boss, but I should know that any man who threatens with an uncocked automatic isn't smart enough to work for himself. Somebody else pulled the strings — Baldy just pulls the trigger.

"We're gonna let you off at the next corner," said Baldy. "But you gotta promise to be good."

"On a stack of Bibles," I said. "Can I have my gun."

"You gotta be kidding?"

"Yeah," I said. "I'm kidding."

They let me out and I watched as the limo went east.

As soon as it turned the corner, I took out my note pad and jotted down the license number.

I took a streetcar back to my office, feeling as stupid as the nickel thugs who tried to intimidate me. There was something about them that was terribly unprofessional. Professionals would have left an indisputably clear message that I was to be off the case, but they wouldn't risk being identified by picking me up and letting me off so I could read the license number of their limousine. It was a Cadillac, and I kept thinking while I was in it that it was the same kind of limo the fake Charlotte Randolph was in when she sped away from Noni's funeral.

By the middle of the afternoon, I tracked down Kansas and asked him to have dinner with me at Cristo's. The cuisine is Italian, and I like the veal, but when Kansas goes to an Italian restaurant, all he can think of is spaghetti and meat balls. I think he learned that in the army.

"You're going to ask me questions about the Noni Light case again, right?" Kansas said, while we waited for our food.

"Right."

"You know, I don't have much of an education, but I ain't stupid. I like you, Kane, but you're making me nervous on this one."

I waited until he finished swallowing his Chianti before I asked him, "How?"

"You're asking too many questions. Makes me think you're just trying to find out what I know."

"What do you know?"

"See what I mean?"

The hefty Italian waitress brought my lasagna and Kansas' spaghetti and the Kansas tucked his red napkin behind his collar. He probably learned *that* when he was a kid.

"How many cases have we been on together?" I said.

"We've been on no cases together – you've stuck your nose in dozens," he said.

"And on how many do I ask you questions?"

"All of 'em," he said.

"Than why is this one making you nervous?"

"It's the first one I remember you admitting being at the scene of the crime."

"So you suspect me. You wouldn't be a cop if you didn't. On how many others did you suspect me?"

"Most."

"So why don't you just keep giving me information, I'll keep solving your case for you and we'll get along just fine."

Kansas was sucking in a long strand of spaghetti. After it was in his mouth, he took a couple of chews, and waved his fork at me while his elbow rested on the table. "Sometimes you test friendship just a little bit too much."

"You know the local mobsters. Right?"

He nodded.

"You know a big bald guy who hangs out with a dark-haired guy who looks like he barely missed making it in the movies? They drive a Cadillac limo."

Kansas chopped a meatball in half with his fork, stuffed it in his mouth, chewed and started twirling another ball of spaghetti. He was being very careful with his food, but I could tell he was thinking.

"Lots of mobsters hang out with good looking henchman types. It brings in the broads."

Kansas shoved the ball of spaghetti into his mouth and started to chew, but he was still thinking. He spoke again after he swallowed. "Cornie DiRisio is big and he hangs with this guy who puts you in mind of Robert Taylor. They scoot around town in twin red Jaguars. It's only in the movies that mobsters use limousines. L.A. mobsters anyhow. Everybody out here goes Hollywood."

I remember seeing a couple of red Jaguars playing tag in the traffic a few times, and I thought about the guys in the limo. These guys were definitely not Jaguar types. They'd never have that much fun.

"Anybody else?" I said.

"Nobody who sounds like your guys."

I nodded. I knew they'd show up again. I only hoped I saw them before they saw me. "Did you locate any parents for Noni Light?" I asked.

"Studio did. They invited them out here to meet the stars. Then they'll let 'em take whatever they want from her apartment."

"Real big hearted of them. When?"

"Next weekend maybe."

"You got any real clues?"

"Your fingerprints," he said. "But somebody else was in there with gloves. The corpse left a diary that sounds more like a storybook than the real thing. If you believe what she put in it, she's screwed just about every big name in Hollywood."

"It's possible," I said.

"She even claims she screwed Roger Francene, and everybody but his fans knows he's a fairy."

"You do have a classic way of putting things," I said.

"Hey, look, I call 'em the way I see 'em. A guy who likes other guys is a fairy."

"You talk to Lester Randolph yet?"

"How did you know about Randolph?" Kansas said.

"I followed 'em both for two weeks, remember?"

"You think he killed her?" Kansas said.

"He might have wanted to get rid of her, but that wasn't a good enough reason to make her dead."

"Except maybe he didn't want his wife to know."

"It happens all the time out here. It usually ends up in a messy divorce, not murder," I said. "Did you find Lydia Lane yet?"

"Yeah. She don't know nothin' either."

When a lot of people don't know anything, somebody's

hiding something. I toyed with the idea of giving Kansas everything I knew. He had more foot-power than I did, and he might get to the bottom of Noni Light's murder a lot quicker if I gave him a head start. But somebody in his department would screw it up. I decided to hold back a few things.

"I'll give you the names of people who are involved with her," I said, and I went down the list one name at a time.

He kept asking me what I thought, but I said he'd be better off if he weren't prejudiced by what I said.

"Not a bad idea," he said, and he kept writing in his notebook. "You got a lot of names here."

"That's all they are, just names."

"What am I supposed to do with them?"

"Whatever works," I said, "and I want you to do me a favor."

"Like what?"

I gave him the tag number of Baldy and Jeeve's limousine and asked him if he could find out who owned it.

"What do you want to know for?"

"Little research for a job I'm doing." It was a prepared answer, but I was glad he didn't follow up with another question.

He looked curiously at the tag number for a moment. Then he shrugged. "You gave me something, I'll get you something," he said.

I started off the next morning by driving out to Regal Studios. Regal wasn't as big as MGM or Morgan, it hardly even beat Republic, but it did a booming trade in B-movies, and that kept them in business. Timothy Shaughnesy, studio guard *extraordinare*, peered into my Ford as I pulled halfway through the front gate.

"Well there, Mr. Kane. What are you doin' on Poverty Row so early in the mornin'?" he said with the lilt of a man who was proud of his heritage.

"Miss Hastings here yet?"

"She come in real early. They're shootin' one of them there scientifical things, kind of like *King Kong*, only it's a big bug. She should be finishin' up pretty soon."

"You mind if I drive through?"

"Well, you surely don't have a pass," he said, "but Mr. Clarke says you're welcome on the lot here anytime. So you can go straight on back and around to the left. They're shootin' on the big sound stage. Her rooms are on the first floor of the Green Building."

"Thanks," I said. Green was the color as well as the name of the building.

I drove slowly and carefully. The Regal lot wasn't full of people in period costumes the way you'd see down at MGM or Morgan, but I saw two cowboy's and three Indians in front of a lunch wagon. I also saw two men in silver coveralls, carrying what looked like fish bowls that were probably supposed to be space helmets.

As I approached the Green Building, with its rows of expensive cars parked out front, Gloria Hastings stepped into the bright haze. She had the narrow face and high cheekbones of a fashion model. Her red hair curved in gentle waves and she wore the kind of simple yellow dress that might be worn by one of the girls from the typing pool. Before I could get to her, she climbed behind the wheel of a pre-war Lincoln Continental convertible, one of the ones with the covered spare tire over the rear bumper.

"Miss Hastings," I called, and I got out of my car.

She tilted her head forward and looked over the top of her

dark glasses.

"Do I know you?" she said.

"Name's Kane, I'm looking into the murder of Noni Light."

"The little slut," she said, looking up at me. "You a cop?"

"No," I said. I would have been happy to let her make the assumption if she hadn't asked the question.

She smiled too broadly. "Just a private *dick*, right?"

"Right," I said.

"Yeah, I've seen you around here before. I don't have to answer to you, do I?"

"You don't have to," I said.

"Did Bobby say I had to?" She was referring to Robert Regal Clarke, the head of the studio.

"No," I said.

"Then I won't," she said, her smile broadening to the point of sarcasm. "Get your car out of my way."

"Yes, ma'am," I said, adding a little sarcasm of my own. No sooner had I backed back my Ford out of the way then she zoomed her car in reverse, spun the wheel hard and backed alongside me.

"How bad do you want the information?" she yelled across her top-down convertible.

"It would help me a hell of a lot," I said.

"You think so, huh?" She sucked in on her cheeks, emphasizing the bone structure of her face. I saw her in a lot of Westerns and she always looked good, but I never before realized the coquette side of her. She always played the wife of some farmer, the school marm or the sad, dance hall sweetheart with a heart of gold. The last picture I saw her in, she played a lady scientist.

"You can have all the information you want," she said, smiling. "All you have to do is catch me."

Before I could speak again, she floored the Continental and zoomed toward the front gate.

CHAPTER 10

Gloria Hastings' Continental squealed around the corner of the sound stage as I followed her. She was one of the two most important actresses on the lot. She could run-down two cowboys or a tribe of Indians if she wanted, and still suffer no more than a slap on the wrist from Bobby Clarke. I had just done a lot of work for him, so I had to be careful. If I had an accident here, I could not only lose my studio privileges, but worse – all the work Clarke threw my way.

By the time I negotiated through the people and props to the studio main street, Gloria Hastings was through the gates and turning right.

"That there was Miss Hastings," Shaughnessy called, pointing as I pulled even with the guard station.

"Thanks," I shouted, and I made the turn.

She turned left at the next street, and I was after her. She weaved down roads and up streets, reached Ventura Boulevard and started West. Every time I closed the gap she increased her speed. I pulled back and so did she, and I realized she didn't care about the speed, it was not getting caught that was important to her.

Her car had far more power than mine, and I didn't think I'd catch her, but I kept trying. I expected her to turn down

Sepulveda. Instead, she kept going west, zooming through Encino and Tarzana. I stayed with her, and she finally turned toward Malibu at Topanga Canyon. On my car radio, Frankie Laine started to scream "Mule Train" and crack his whip. I had trouble following Gloria Hastings along the winding road.

"Clippity clop, clippity clop, clippity cloppin' along . . . Yah . . ." he sang, and the whip cracked. "Mule Traaaaaaain . . ." Frankie Laine and I screamed together.

Gloria Hastings lost me again, and each time she did, I expected to find her Continental smashed into the canyon wall or crashed through a broken guard rail at the next turn. Instead, she kept slowing down to let me catch up. It was a game, and all she wanted was to win. In her mind that meant keeping me from catching her until she was damn good and ready to be caught, or until she wanted to leave me in the dust.

She turned West at Malibu, and I continued to follow her until she swung hard into the driveway of one of the beachfront houses. She was already unlocking the side door of the house as I skidded to a halt in the cinders.

I jumped out of my car and reached her just in time to get my foot slammed in the door.

"Damn!" I shouted, edging my shoulder inside.

"You didn't catch me," she said, laughing at me and half-heartedly pushing her weight against the door.

"Wanna bet?" I said, and I pushed hard, forcing my way inside. I looked straight into her green eyes, and she peeled her lips back against the white of her clenched teeth.

"Now what?" she said, pursing her lips in a challenge.

I put my arms around her and pulled her to me, planting my mouth on hers. Our teeth clicked against each other's. At first she resisted. Then she opened her mouth wide and bit down hard on my tongue. I pulled away, tasting my own blood.

"What the hell'd you do that for?" I said.

She put her hand inside my collar, snapping the top button and loosening the tie in the same motion.

"*Just* for the hell of it," she said.

She kissed me hard and probed my mouth with her tongue as she continued to loosen the tie. I still tasted the blood as she slipped her fingers away and ripped the buttons down the front of my shirt. Then, sneering, she drew her nails down my chest, again drawing blood. I pushed her hard against the wall of the foyer and bit down on her neck.

"Not the neck! It'll show," she whispered in panic. As soon as I stopped, she planted her mouth on my neck and bit hard. I slid my hands under her skirt, passing them roughly over the snaps of her garter belt to the silk of her panties.

"Yes, yes. Tear it. Tear it," she said, through clenched teeth.

I ripped away at the silk while she yanked down on my zipper. Roughly, she freed my erection from the poplin trousers. Then she put her arms behind my back and brought both hands up to my shoulders to support herself. She drew herself up the front of my body and impaled herself on me.

"Ohhhhh, yes!" she cried, as if in relief, and she wrapped her legs around me.

I pressed her against the wall, and she writhed at me. She searched for my lips with her own. When she found them, she sucked hard at my breath and drew her legs ever more tightly around me.

"Ooooo," she moaned, and I was slamming her against the wall, both of us grunting. Her right hand was under the back of my jacket, and her sharp nails ripped through my shirt, dragging like dull razors across the flesh of my back. I wrapped my arms around her, one under her buttocks, the other behind her back. She continued to writhe as I stepped away from the wall and carried her, still wrapped around me, into the living room.

I pushed away the ash tray and cigarette lighter with my knee, and lowered her to the surface of the cocktail table. Her legs pointed upward, and I continued to thrust and withdraw. Her moans became cries, her cries – screeches. She screamed again and again, and I continued to work harder and harder until I was finally and fully spent.

Then I let out my own sigh of relief, dropped my weight on her, and rested. After a moment, I leaned up on my hands and looked down into her satisfied smile. Her green eyes were framed in bloodshot red. Her mouth was smeared with her own lipstick.

"I could have you arrested for this, you know," she said.

"Sure you could," I said.

I pushed away from her and flopped into a yellow canvas easy chair. After a few seconds, she swung around and sat on the edge of the cocktail table. She had a cigarette between her fingers, but I had no idea where she got it. I unsnapped my Zippo and lit it for her.

"Who the hell are you anyhow?" she said, after she inhaled.

"I told you: name's Kane, private detective."

"I don't know how private you are," she said. "Let's go for a swim."

She got me a pair of oversized bathing trunks. I felt like a fool and drew the strings as tight as they would go, but they were so big, I looked like some kid. Gloria looked gorgeous in her yellow bikini. Her breasts didn't seem as large as when she was wearing clothes, but they were shaped just fine. The cheeks of her buttocks wiggled at me as she hopped off the porch, darted across the sand, and dove into the surf.

The sun had broken through the haze, and I swam after her as far as the breakers. I never caught her until we were back into the shallow water. I was only halfway through explaining what I was doing on the case when she got excited and pulled down on my loose bathing trunks.

Seconds after that, we were making love in the surf. She seemed unconcerned what her neighbors might see or think. After all, Malibu and Hollywood were just the suburbs of Sodom and Gomorrah, and Caligula's Rome. We hurried back to the house and made love in the shower. Then we toweled each other dry.

"Don't you ever quit?" she said, while she fixed me Johnny Walker Black and water.

She didn't seem to quit either, I thought, but I said, "I'm finished for the time being," and tasted my drink.

She was wore a dark green robe and dangled a glass of white wine between her forefinger and thumb. She had one of those silly little smiles some women wear after good sex.

My guess was that all of her sex was good. She looked very coy leaning back in the corner of the yellow canvas sofa that was obviously made for bathers. She stayed that way, staring and smiling for a long time. Finally, she tasted her wine.

"Now, what can you tell me about Noni Light?" I said.

"With men, it's always business, isn't it?"

She cocked her head slightly to the side, hiding her face behind the glass.

"Noni was a nice kid. If she'd played her cards right, she could've been a star."

"Yeah. Sure," I said. "How should she have played her cards?"

"Ah . . ." Gloria squinched up her nose. "Noni tried to make her points with the wrong people. You know: Lester and Toby. She was even playing up to that old fart Louie Mayer, and he doesn't have anything to do with that studio anymore. Not really."

"Wasn't Noni under contract to Morgan."

"She's been under contract to Morgan since she was fifteen

and her seven years were just about up."

"Got any idea who killed her?"

Gloria sloshed her wine in the big glass and tasted it.

"Well?" I said.

Finally, she looked up. "Roger Francene," she said.

"Why him?"

Naming Roger confused me. After she gave the reason, I was even more confused, and it must have shown on my face.

"How much do you know about him?" she said.

"I know he's a homosexual, if that's what you mean."

"He is and he isn't. It's according to his mood. But you're right. Mostly, he likes men, young men. But when he has to settle for a girl, he's not a bad lover."

"You know from personal experience?"

"I do. He can be as nice as an old-maid aunt or as bitchy as a wicked step-mother. It's all according to how he feels."

She tasted her wine again, and I tasted my Johnny Walker.

"Did you know he's Lester's brother-in-law?" she said.

I didn't know, but it explained something that was bugging me. When I saw him without movie make-up and no elevator shoes, I knew there was something about him that was familiar. It was the family resemblance.

"He's Charlotte Randolph's brother?" I asked, just to make sure he wasn't the brother-in-law by a route I didn't know about.

"Yep. Him and Charlotte were child actors together. She wasn't bad in the movies, but when she met Lester, and when she had the second kid, she decided not to go back to the screen. Do you know her?"

"I've met her," I said.

"I don't like her. She thinks she's better than the rest of us."

If I disliked everybody who fit that description, there wouldn't be a lot of people in Hollywood I could stand. "How does she show it?" I asked.

Gloria did the squinched nose thing again. "She doesn't recognize Hollywood for what it is: just one big orgy. You know, I think she'd actually get upset if she heard Lester was dipping his wick into every starlet on the Morgan lot."

"You don't think she knows?"

"If she does, she keeps it a damn good secret. When she goes to a party, she sticks to him like she doesn't have another friend in the world. When some little bitch comes up to him and makes googly eyes, she just smirks."

"What should she do?"

"At least show some kind of upset. I mean, crap, if a little chickie comes up to a guy I'm with, I get steamed. I might even get jealous of you if I knew you better. She's not natural."

In a sense, I understood what she meant. The natural thing for Hollywood was to screw around whether you were married or not. The unnatural thing was to keep your kids at home, send them to a local school, and act like a real mother. Even the people out here who stayed married left their kids at home with a nanny or sent them off to some school – the farther away the better. For a moment, I thought of Charlotte standing in front of me in that gray robe. Then I realized both my mind and body were off the subject.

"You said Roger would kill Noni because he liked her too much?" I said.

"Noni's one of those sweet little things that fairies love to love."

"Homosexuals?"

"What are you a prude? You know what I mean."

I knew.

"She liked to hang out with them, you know. They treated her like a princess. Roger didn't mind himself hanging with her and treating her that way, but when she started to go out with some of his boy friends, he put a stop to it."

"How?"

"He told them to lay off."

"Are you telling me that Lester and Toby . . ."

"Hell, no! Those guys don't have a sensitive bone in their bodies. Roger introduced her to them to keep her in the right frame of reference. You see, he wasn't jealous of guys who wanted to screw her, it was only other faggots that he was jealous of – and I'm not sure if he was jealous of them or her."

"You got some kind of degree in psychology?"

I drained my glass of all but ice. She took the glass away from me and to the liquor cabinet for a refill. While she was gone, I tried to sort out what she had just told me. In a vague, perverted way, it made sense.

If Noni was with other homosexual men, he was jealous because he was homosexual, and Roger knew they thought of her the same way he did, and they were intruding on his territory. Not for sex necessarily but . . . Now, I was losing my train of thought. None of it made sense, because I had no idea how those guys thought.

Gloria handed me a fresh Johnny and water and dangled a refill of wine in front of her.

"You're not telling me he used her to pull in young men who . . ."

"Hell no. Are you kidding? A guy with a reputation like Roger's can have his pick of any interested boy in Hollywood. Noni was like a boy who slept around and sometimes . . ."

"You're saying he liked both men and women?" I said.

"Boys and girls," she said correcting me.

"Children?" I said with disgust.

"That's not Roger's style. He likes them in their late teens, early twenties, already adults, but a bit immature. That's why he dropped me a couple of years ago." She laughed through her nose. "I was his Noni before Noni," she said.

"Who's his Noni now?"

"This is starting to sound like a Danny Kaye routine," she said, laughing. "I don't know yet, but I suspect it's one of Noni's good friends. What's her name? Lydia something-or-other?"

I nodded. I knew she was talking about Lydia Lane. From what I knew now, that might make some sense, but I still wasn't buying it.

"You think she's in danger?" I said.

"If she behaves herself and leaves Roger's boy friends alone, everything'll be fine."

"How come nothing ever happened to you?"

"He was my one and only faggot," she said, fluttering her eyelashes in mockery. She relished using that word and words like it. She was still angry at him for dropping her.

"How long did it last? You and Roger?"

She tasted her wine and smirked. "Till the last year or so. He got Noni and he dropped me. 'No hard feelings,' he said."

"How about you?"

"Jealous of a faggot? You got to be kidding?"

Sure, I thought. All she did was imply he was guilty of murder. "How long were you with him? How many years?"

"Who are you working for anyhow?" she said, and she tasted her wine.

"Myself." She was another one whose photo I might get with Lester Randolph to prove his infidelity, and I didn't want to tip her off that I was also working for Charlotte.

"Not Bobby Clarke?"

I shook my head. She tried to pump me for details, but she got nothing. The most I told her was that I liked Noni, and I didn't like the fact that she had been murdered.

"The avenging angel," she said, smirking and dangling the glass some more.

"I don't like to see anybody murdered. Especially people I know. I might even take the same attitude if somebody killed you."

"Now that you know me?" She tasted her wine again and stared at me over the rim of the glass, the flash of a smile in her green eyes.

"Now that I know you," I said, with mock assurance.

I wanted to try one more time for the answer to that question about how long she had been "with" Roger Francene, but I didn't want to press my luck. So far, I was still on her good side.

"What did you think of Noni?" I said.

"I liked her. Nice kid."

"How well did you know her?"

"We were at some parties together."

"Were you friends?"

"What are you getting at?" she said.

"Just wanted to know if you were friends," I said.

"That might be stretching it, but I felt bad about her getting killed."

"Not bad enough to go to her funeral?"

"Are you looking for a fight?"

"Just checking on things."

She looked at me curiously, like she didn't want to answer my questions, but didn't want to appear uncooperative either. She sighed and leaned back.

"You've seen my movies, right?"

I nodded.

"Then you know the goody-goody image I've got on screen. A sweet thing like me shows up at a funeral for some bleached-blond tramp, and before you know it, Bobby Clarke pulls my contract. He's always trying to find new parts for Hanna Mills."

Her expression turned very smug, and she spoke again, "Besides, it was a Morgan funeral."

"Gable and Mayer were there."

"And I thought you were a Hollywood insider," she teased. "Didn't you know she made love to both of them?"

"I'm not an insider. I'm just a detective who hangs around, but I thought Louie Mayer was more like a father than a lover?"

She shrugged, which probably meant she didn't know.

"You don't suspect me of anything do you?" she said, raising her eyebrows.

"Kiddo, I suspect everybody."

I drained my glass for the last time – at least the last time today. Then I stood and looked down at her.

She wasn't very happy right now. "You looking for a fight?" she said. She rose and sneered. It wasn't a fight she wanted – not in the traditional sense.

"I'd love to give you a fight. But I've got some things to do."

"More important than fighting with me?" she said, stepping toward me and moving her face within inches of mine.

"Only for the time being."

With her robe drawn tightly around her, she reminded me of Charlotte Randolph, and I had to get out of there before Gloria got me interested again.

I still didn't know what happened to Kitty.

CHAPTER 11

As soon as I was home, I called Kitty. When I got no answer, I called her service. They told me she had been expected today and that she hadn't returned to the area yet, but that they would take a message.

Kitty never went anyplace without saying something to me about it, and that worried me even more. People don't act one way for six years and suddenly change for no reason.

It just wasn't like her.

I never thought I'd do something like this, but just after dark, I drove to Kitty's two-bedroom house near Beverly Hills.

I parked my car a couple of streets away and sneaked across the lawns to the front door. An outsider might think I was acting like a cuckolded lover. If I were objective, I might see it that way too, but I just wasn't comfortable with her disappearing and not telling me where she went.

There were no lights in the house as I stepped up on the porch and opened the mailbox. I took out my penlight and looked at postmarks. It looked like she hadn't picked up her mail since Saturday, but if what they told me at the modeling agency was true, she didn't go to work on Monday either.

I thought about the nickel hoods who tried to hassle me, and I wondered if they might have anything to do with the fact that Kitty was gone. The more I wondered, the more I worried. Baldy and his glamour-boy henchman seemed more crazy than efficient. In some respects, it made them more dangerous.

I took out the set of picks I commandeered a couple of years ago and jimmied the lock. I hoped like hell that Kitty would never find out, because she valued her privacy, and I wasn't sure she'd forgive me.

Her place was more elegantly decorated than the last time she let me come there. Everything was new and more expensive. There was a tin of caviar in the new refrigerator and almost everything else was more to a connoisseur's taste than I remembered. It even occurred to me that I might have the wrong house, but this was Kitty's place all right.

I flashed my light over to her bedroom and carefully opened the drawers of her desk. I found her bankbook and hesitated before looking at it. If she were just anybody it wouldn't bother me at all, but she was Kitty, my best friend, the person whose company I enjoyed more than anyone else in the world. It was an absolute invasion of privacy, but it was necessary. I actually took a deep breath before I flipped back the fake-leather cover of the bankbook.

"Jesus!" I muttered.

Kitty had well over thirty thousand dollars in her savings account. Most of it had been put there in the last two years. Just after the first of each of the last twenty-three months, she deposited in the neighborhood of fifteen hundred dollars. I put the bankbook away and rummaged some more. I found a stack of stock certificates, most in blue chips like AT&T, but there were certificates in something called International Business Machines, a company I didn't know. In another drawer there was over a thousand dollars in cash. Kitty was doing very well for herself, and she wasn't making that much as a model. I felt like I was betraying her even more when I read the copy of her will, leaving everything to me, including the money in the bank, the house, and even the red M.G.

When I started to go through her underwear drawer, I came up with a "date book," that listed some of the biggest names in Hollywood, including Toby Wentworth and Lester Randolph. Roger Francene's name was not there. I felt even worse because I had intruded into her business life, which spilled over into her personal life, and I was part of that.

At least, in a sense, I was part of it.

As best I could, I put everything back where I found it, slipped out of the house, and went back to my own apartment.

I called Kitty's service and got a different operator, but the message hadn't changed: Kitty would not get back to anyone for a few days. I asked if there was a particular message for me and the operator said there wasn't.

I was worried, and I called police headquarters, but Kansas was gone for the day. I left a message for him to call me in the morning.

I called his apartment, but there was no answer. I went to bed and thought of some of the things Lydia said about the party, but I must have fallen asleep immediately.

"Kane?" It was Kitty's voice, and I jumped up from what I thought was a deep sleep.

"Kitty," I said. I swung my feet to the floor and hurried through the apartment. My name, spoken in Kitty's voice, had sounded so clear.

"Kitty!" I called again.

When I looked in every corner of my apartment, I realized it was a dream, but it was still hard to believe. I tossed for about twenty minutes, but it was impossible to sleep, so I called Lydia Lane.

"It's me, Brian Kane," I said. "I want to come over."

"It's three o'clock in the morning, for crap sake," she said, but she was more surprised than objecting.

"I know, but it's important," I said.

I knew she lived in the same building as Noni and the women were not allowed guests after ten o'clock, but I insisted. Lydia gave me directions to her French windows that overlooked the pool in the back of the apartments.

Her directions were clear, but she gave me a hint. "Just in case you think it's the wrong place," she said. "I got a little piece of tape on the bottom middle pain of glass of the right door."

"Is the place patrolled."

"Sometimes."

The song went through my mind all the way to her place. "Three O'clock in the Morning . . . We danced the whole night through." As I thought and sometimes whispered the song, I imagined dancing with Kitty and wondered if I'd ever get to dance with her again. I parked the car and worked my way behind the building.

There was a strong breeze, and the water was sloshing against the edge of the pool. When I tapped on the glass of Lydia's apartment, the French doors flew open, and she told me to hurry inside. She looked both ways around the pool as if she thought I might have been followed. Then she clicked the doors closed and leaned her back against it.

A dim light sat on a writing table. With her pink flannel robe over pink flannel pajamas, she seemed more like a little girl than a Morgan starlet. She held her arms around herself as if she were afraid of me.

The apartment was a mirror image on Noni's, and as well as I could figure, Noni's was the one next door.

"I'm sorry I came here so late," I said, "but when's the last time you saw Kitty?"

"Kitty? Oh, I told you – Sunday night, at Toby

Wentworth's party."

She sat demurely on the edge of the sofa that was the same style and print as the one in Noni's apartment. Max Morgan must have got them wholesale.

"What were you doing?" I said.

"At the party? We were having a good time."

"What happened that made you think you needed protection?"

"Nothing," she said, but she bit her lips.

"Was Lester at the party?"

"Yes."

"Who with?"

She didn't answer.

"It's clear he wasn't with you. Was he with Kitty?" Again, she didn't answer, but I wasn't sure she meant yes.

"Did she go home with him?"

"No."

"Who did she go home with?"

"By herself, she left by herself."

"And you?"

"Together, we left together."

"Was she by herself or were you together? Which?"

"Together. We went to her place. She dropped me off at your office in the morning."

"Why did you go to her place?"

"I was afraid. Lester was angry. I was afraid he wanted to kill me. He didn't like it when I showed up at a party where he was. Especially when I was with somebody else."

"Who?"

Again, she didn't want to answer. I zipped up a Camel, inhaled and waited. I would have done one for her, but I remembered she didn't smoke.

"I was with Toby," she said.

"Did Lester threaten you?"

"He didn't have to. It was the way he looked at me. You've seen him in the movies. You know what he's like when he gets mad. You know that look. He could kill you just looking at you like that."

"Did he threaten you?"

"No. It was just the look, that God-awful look."

"Has he ever killed anybody before?"

"Not that I know of. Except in the army."

I inhaled, then let out a long stream of smoke. As far as I knew, Lester Randolph had never been in the army. But during the war, I didn't follow the career of every actor in Hollywood. I was too busy getting my ass surrounded by the Nazis at Bastogne. I thought I saw a few wartime movies with Lester Randolph in them, but I might be wrong.

"Have you talked to him since you saw me yesterday?"

She said "No," but she was too quick with it.

"When did he call?"

She was silent again. This time, I didn't push. I just waited and inhaled.

"He wanted me to come see him on his boat," she said.

"Didn't you already spend some time with him on the boat over the weekend?"

"How'd you know that?"

"I'm a detective. Remember?"

She remembered, but she was confused. She had no idea that I was following Lester for a couple of weeks, unless Kitty told her, and that wouldn't be like Kitty.

"Lets try this again: have you seen him since Sunday?"

"Yes," she said, and I assumed she meant after she talked to me yesterday.

"Why?"

"I don't know."

"Aren't you still afraid of him?"

"Yes."

It was going to be hard to protect her against a man she thought was going to kill her if she kept going to him. Maybe there was no threat at all. Maybe she and Randolph were setting me up for something. Or maybe she was just paranoid.

"When's the last time you saw Kitty?"

"Monday morning. After we spent the night at her place."

"Was she driving her own car?"

"She was driving a little red thing."

That would be Kitty's M.G.

"She just let you off and left?" I said. "Was she the one who let you in my office?" Kitty did have a key. She had all my keys.

"No. She said you always showed up to look at the mail, and you would be there at nine o'clock. She drove away and said she was gonna go back to her apartment. Your office was open when I went in."

"You're lying to me," I said. "You didn't spend the whole night at her place."

"I did. Honest I did."

"Kitty doesn't have an apartment. She had a house,"

I said *had*, and I realized I was talking about Kitty in the past tense. "Where did you spend the night?"

"Are you going to protect me or just yell at me?" she said, and she broke down into tears.

"Where?"

She looked down and mumbled a name.

"Who?"

"Lester's boat," she said.

I had already imagined them with Toby Wentworth and I refused to imagine them with Lester. I had no right to question Kitty about what she did with her time, but I was afraid of what might have happened to her.

"You left Lester's boat together?"

"Yes," she said. "She let me into your office, and she said she was going home."

That at least explained how Lydia got in, but I was convinced Kitty never went back to her house. If not, where did she go? And why did she leave messages at the modeling agency and the answering service that she would be out of town for a few days? Maybe it was all true, but I still wasn't comfortable. I snubbed my Camel in the fake crystal ashtray, and looked up at her.

"I don't know where she went," Lydia said, and the look in her eyes told me she was worried for me.

I had a cup of very old coffee. Then I slipped out of Lydia's apartment. She watched through the curtain for a while.

In a few minutes, I doubled back and broke into Noni's apartment next door. It was exactly as I remembered it, including the ash tray with the twin pelicans crossing their beaks.

In the bedroom, there was a crude chalk outline where her body had fallen on the Persian rug. There was also a chalk circle that marked a single small item. It might be the outline of a spent shell, except that Noni was not shot with an automatic weapon. I stooped and flashed my pen light on the small circle. A lipstick case? But it was too far from the dressing table to have rolled there. Her pocket book might have fallen open, but there was no mark for a pocket book.

"Tell me about the lipstick case you found in Noni Light's apartment," I asked Kansas when I showed up at his office at City Hall. He had a lot of scraps of paper laid out on his desk, and he was studying them as if they were pieces of a jig-saw puzzle.

"You were snooping around there, weren't you?" he said, looking up.

"Me?"

He reached in the top right hand corner of his desk, took one of those ugly smelling cigars, lit it up, and leaned back in his chair, crossing his arms in front of him.

"Yeah, you," he said. "Sometimes I think I should just give you a badge."

"Then I couldn't snoop around."

Kansas grunted something between a laugh and a chuckle. He thought for a moment and came to a decision.

"Lipstick didn't belong to her," he said.

"How do you know?"

"Wrong color. It was pale, almost pink."

The fake Mrs. Randolph wore pale lipstick. So did Kitty. So did Gloria Hastings.

"I'm worried about Kitty," I said.

"Changing the subject so quick?"

It was the subject I should have started with. I explained about what the answering service was telling me. "She's gone away before, but she always told me about it before she left."

"You got it better than a whole lot of marriages. What are you worried about?"

He was right about that, but like a most marriages, there were worries. I thought about the nickel hoods like Baldy and Jeeves and I wondered if they had any connection with Kitty being missing.

"Did you get an I.D. on that tag number I gave you?"

"There you go changing the subject again," he said, and he sighed. He slid open the top drawer of his desk and pulled out a slip of paper. "Limousine's registered to the Warner Brothers

Studio. Reported stolen last week."

If it had been Regal or Morgan or even MGM, there might be a connection, but so far nobody connected this case had anything to do with Warner Brothers.

"You okay?" said Kansas.

"Yeah, fine."

"Are you *that* worried about her?"

"You know me. I don't worry about anything," I said.

"You and her need a vacation. Why don't you take her down to Mexico or something?"

"Sure," I said, and I forced a smile.

I'd be happy to take a vacation with Kitty – anytime, anywhere.

But now what I had to do was find her safe.

CHAPTER 12

I kept telling myself that Kitty was okay, but I wasn't convinced. At the same time, I thought about every missing-persons case I had ever handled. The husband or the wife was absolutely certain the mate had fallen victim to foul play, but in nine cases out of ten, it was just somebody playing around outside the marriage. I hated to think it was that way with Kitty, but in a sense, it might be true. Kitty, after all, was an expensive call girl. What did I expect: fidelity? Of course not. I just wanted to be sure she was safe.

I should just stop thinking about her. She'd eventually show up with no need for an excuse and everything would be fine.

At least, that's what I told myself.

I called Kitty's answering service, then her house, but there was still no good news. Then I called over to the Morgan Studios to try to get in touch with Lester Randolph.

"I'm sorry, but Mr. Randolph is not on the lot today."

"Was he there yesterday?"

"No, sir?"

"Monday?"

"If you want to know more about Mr. Randolph, I think it would be best if you talked to his secretary."

"That won't be necessary," I said, and I called over to Warners.

I asked for the person who reported the stolen limousine. After being transferred through four repeated lines of "One moment please", I got the same wrong person three different times, I was finally connected to a woman who sounded as if she hummed her words through something like a kazoo.

"Yes, mmmmm. I'm the one you want to speak to about that, but I don't have time now. Perhaps this afternoon would be better, mmmmm?"

Only the last "mmmmm" was a question.

"This afternoon will be fine," I said.

I closed up my office and drove over to the marina where Lester Randolph tied his boat, but the boat was not at the pier. Maybe that meant Kitty was safe, I thought as I drove toward the Randolph's house. When I arrived, Charlotte was just leaving.

She wore a plane white dress and carried a white purse as she climbed into the driver's seat of her yellow Jaguar convertible. It was a huge car, low and curved, but with only enough room for a driver and one passenger. As I pulled up behind her in the circular driveway, I wondered why anyone would own such a car. I beeped my horn, and she looked over her shoulder. I got out of my Ford and walked up to her.

"I was hoping to talk to you," I said. It was really her husband I wanted to talk to, but she might be able to fill me in on a couple of things.

She looked up at me and smiled. "I'd like to thank you again for pulling my little girl out of the pool."

"Anybody would have done it."

"I know, but you're the one that did," she said. "I'd like to talk with you a little bit, but I've got an appointment to get my hair done."

"Your husband in?"

"He's been gone for a few days," she said. "Away with one

of his bitches, no doubt."

I bristled, thinking that "one of his bitches" might be Kitty, and I wanted to come to her defense, but that would be even more stupid than some things I had already done.

I nodded and smiled, not necessarily in agreement.

"I won't be long. If you'd like to meet me in a couple of hours, we can have a drink and, uh, and talk."

"Where?" I said.

"How about Moonset?" she said. It was a place on Sunset Boulevard, and not far from my office.

"Very intimate. Very dark," she said, with mock seduction.

I told her I knew the place.

"See you in two hours?" she said. She fanned her fingers at me, drew them into a fist, and drove away.

I stopped back at my office to check the afternoon mail. Among the pieces that had been shoved under my door was a manila envelope bordered in red, with an Encino post mark.

Out of curiosity, I opened it first, unwinding the little red string. I found something I neither expected nor wanted: six, eight by ten glossy photos of Kitty. She was naked and posed very poorly, alone on a bed. Her arms and legs were spread at various angles, revealing intimate details. Her eyes were open in only one of the photos, and it appeared that she was either very drunk or on drugs. But at least she was alive.

It was only after I looked at all six of the photos that I saw the note on lavender paper, which read: "We told you to stay out of Noni Light's business. If you're lucky, you get this one back alive."

Sons of bitches, I thought, and I dialed Police Headquarters. I was determined to get Kansas to help me on this, but the guy on the switchboard told me he was out. Whoever killed Noni was serious about getting me off the case, but they played me backwards.

Nobody ever scared me off a case – they just made me work harder, and I would work doubly hard to find Kitty. I thought about Lydia's fear of Lester Randolph, I thought about the fact that his boat was apparently out to sea, and I thought about the fact that I had a date to meet Randolph's wife. The first step to finding Randolph, and therefore Kitty, might be to talk to Charlotte, and I was going to do that soon.

Coming out of the sunlight into the interior darkness of Moonset was like stepping suddenly into blindness. The first thing I did was to bump into Seppi, the maitre d'.

"Yeah?" said Seppi.

"I'm meeting somebody," I said.

"Oh. Hi, Mr. Kane. You meetin' a lady?"

"Yes."

"I'll give you a boot," he said, meaning "booth."

I saw L.A. cops here on their off hours, and I saw people from organized crime, but I never saw them together. Moonset was not the kind of place where the normal Hollywood crowd hung out, but you saw them there occasionally, looking as if they were trying to hide from the world.

Seppi led me to a booth in the far corner of the room. When the waiter came, I ordered Scotch on the rocks. At Moonset, there was no sense naming a brand. No matter what you ordered, you always got the bar whiskey.

As my eyes got used to the dark, I saw there were other people in the place. Most of them were mixed couples in booths, whose faces were obscure. Some were eating. Some were just talking. I tried eating here before, but I don't like food I can't see.

About fifteen minutes later, I saw a white dress and a man's shirt floating across the floor through the darkness.

"Here he is," said the Seppi. His was the white shirt.

"Thank you," said Charlotte Randolph, and she slid in the seat across from me. Her hair was different now, pushed all the way to one side. Normally, she was a gorgeous woman. In the darkness of Moonset, she was just elegant. As if to seal the impression, she ordered a rare cognac. In this instance, I doubted she'd get the bar whiskey, but she wouldn't get what she ordered either.

"Nice to see ya," she said, her rough speech throwing a crack across her impression of worldliness.

I lit us a couple of Camels and put one between her lips.

"I'm not sure Bette Davis'd be impressed, but I am."

She inhaled and exhaled and did that elbow-on-the-table-cigarette-in-the-fist pose that worked so well in the movies.

"Is this the right time?" she said.

"For what?" I said.

"You forgot?"

I hadn't forgotten, but I was thinking about Kitty. My choice now was to keep this line of conversation going with Charlotte or to work on finding Kitty.

"Sorry," I said, pretending to be embarrassed.

"You're shy. I never noticed it before."

"I'm sure there are a lot things you never noticed about me."

She sensed my change, and she too got down to business, but it was the part I wasn't ready for. "Did ya get those pictures of my husband yet?"

"I don't swim well with a camera hanging from my teeth."

"He's on the boat?"

"It's out of dock and nobody can seem to find him, so that's my guess."

The waiter brought her cognac. She tasted it, looking over the rim of the snifter at me, but in the dimness of Moonset, I couldn't really see her eyes. She placed the snifter carefully on the table.

"Who's with him?"

"I don't know," I said, but I had an idea it was Kitty. "I just know who's not with him. Lydia Lane's in town. So is Gloria Hastings."

"Am I paying you for time or the pictures? I forget." She blew smoke across the table at me. I didn't like that.

"Both," I said. "How often does he go out on the water? The two weeks I followed him and Noni, the boat never left the dock.

"Not often," she said. "Lester says it costs a fortune to move it. Says he hardly ever goes out. I only been on the water with him once." She took another sniff and another taste of her cognac.

"Where did he go?"

"Santa Catalina. Parked someplace along the beach and got me to swim nude. I thought that was sexy. Then he thought it was cute to throw chicken guts in the water and watch the sharks come around."

She laughed through her nose.

"I ain't been back on the boat with him yet. He says nobody ever died or lost a leg because of his joke. He thought that was very funny."

I thought of Kitty in the same predicament and it wasn't a pretty picture. "Tell me something," I said. "According to everything I know, you had a happy marriage."

"We did. At least I thought we did, until you sent me that report."

"I told you, I didn't send it."

"Oh, yeah. The lady pretending to be me. I shouldn't blame you, should I? But you gave her the report. Didn't you."

"She hired me to make the report."

"Pretty tricky. You won't give me the report, but you'll give it to her to give to me. What do you call that, uh, honor among thieves?"

She paused and took another taste of her drink.

"You know, I thought I had the happiest marriage in Hollywood." She laughed. "Maybe I did, but I guess that's because I didn't read the columns. Things are really crappy out here. Here, a good marriage is just a dream . . . or a wife like me, kidding herself. Everything out here is just a dream," she trailed off wistfully, staring across the room.

If she were so naive, I wondered how she knew about Moonset, one of the dimmest lit and therefore one of the most discreet haunts on the Sunset Strip. Charlotte started to raise her hand for the waiter, but she changed her mind.

"My children won't be home for a couple of hours yet," she said, raising her chin and swallowing her pride. "Would you like to go to bed with me?"

I'd love to go to bed with her, but Kitty was still missing, and the story about the sharks put an even worse slant on things. I needed more information, and I thought only Lydia could supply it.

"I got a lot to do," I said.

"What?" she said.

"A lot," I said.

"You son of a bitch," she said. "You get me to make a whore out of myself, and you . . ."

"You haven't made an whore out of yourself. You're a very desirable woman, and I want you, but . . ."

"No buts. If you don't go to be with me now, you'll never go to bed with me. You think I can't call somebody else, I —"

I reached across the table and covered her hand with mine. "I'm sorry. Look, I've got a friend who's in trouble. Her life may be in danger."

"A woman?"

"Yes, a woman. A friend."

She paused and thought it over. "When can I see you?" she said. The words were barely audible. She had made a move and I had rebuffed her and she was embarrassed.

"I'll call you."

She looked at me hard. "You son of a bitch," she snarled. "You're saying, 'Don't call me, I'll call you'? Is that what this is all about? You're working for me, remember?"

"I remember. I will see you again. I promise."

I left a ten dollar bill on the table and told her to have another cognac.

"You're fired," she said.

"I'll get your photos anyhow," I said, and I walked away. It was not a good way to leave her, but Kitty was on my mind now. I would not be good at anything except finding her, and I might be too late for that to do any good.

When I stepped outside, the light exploded in my eyes. Even after I put on my sunglasses, I could hardly see.

I waited behind the wheel of my Ford for a few minutes, and Charlotte came out of Moonset. She looked in my direction, but I figured she was as blinded as I was coming out of there, so she couldn't have seen me when she climbed in that yellow land boat of hers and zoomed away.

I followed, wondering if Mrs. Randolph also had a lover on the side, but she went straight back to her house. I was tempted, but I didn't follow onto the circular drive, nor did I park my car outside and go up to her door. Nothing she could tell me would help me find Kitty.

I went to Lydia's apartment building. The desk man told me she had not come back from the studio, but she had called in a phone number where she could be reached.

When I realized it was Roger Francene's number. I thought

about what Gloria Hastings told me about his attachment to Noni, and it made sense.

I went to his house. This time, a good-looking young man in a butler's costume answered the door. His speech was affected but it was a poor imitation of an English accent. Probably another failed actor, I thought, but I also thought of Roger's interest in young men. I told the butler I wanted to see Lydia Lane, but he played stupid. Then I told him I wanted to talk to Roger.

"Mr. Francene doesn't see . . ."

"Tell him it's Kane. I'm investigating the Noni Light murder."

"Oh, yes, Mr. Kane. You can come in," he said, but there was something suspicious about the way he said it. My guess was that he knew who I was when I stepped up to the door, but he was stalling to give Roger time to do something.

He led me into the drawing room, which like the rest of the house, was done in a Tudor style, including the exposed beams. There was a table-like desk with a few books and some papers on top of it and a chair behind it.

Over the fireplace was a tapestry of a foxhunt. In front of it were two easy chairs, one red and one blue, set at angles to a small, round but very sturdy table.

I took the blue chair with the better angle to the door, and when Roger came in, I rose. He stood at all the height his elevator shoes could give him. It was only the shoes that made him taller than his sister.

"You told me you were a policeman!" he said, snarling.

"I told you I was investigating the murder of Noni Light."

"You lead me to believe –"

"You believed what you want to believe. I'd like to speak to Lydia."

"Lydia?"

"Lydia Lane. She left a message that she would be here."

"Oh," he said, as if he just remembered her. "She hasn't arrived yet. She's doing a screen test for Toby. Please sit down."

I raised my eyebrows as I lowered myself back to the blue chair. I thought about the Calamity Jane picture. They probably wouldn't have to test her for a small part. The only reason they'd test her at all would be to consider her for the lead or at least the Belle Starr part. Good for her, I thought. I didn't think she could act, but she wouldn't be the first actress out here to make it without that particular talent.

There was an ash tray on the table so I zipped up a Camel and offered him one, but he waved it off, and I slipped the Zippo back into my pocket.

"Tell me about you and your sister," I said.

"Charlotte?" he said, and he waited for a moment, as if he were considering a lie. Then he spoke again. "We were very close as children, but we don't speak to each other much anymore."

I raised my eyebrows as comment.

"You see, me and Lester . . . Lester and I, are rivals at the box office, so there's a natural competition. And we, me and Lester, don't like each other very much. He doesn't like me being seen with his wife, even if she is my sister. He makes her stay away from me."

Charlotte Randolph did not seem to be the kind of woman who would be intimidated by her husband – or by anyone else for that matter.

"You and Lester are with the same studio. I thought Morgan was just one big happy family. Isn't that's how Max Morgan thinks of it?"

"Max would like to think of it that way, but none of us worry about those old timers anymore. Like Louie Mayer, he's on the way out. Like Dore Schary over at MGM, Dick Wrenking makes all Morgan's decisions. It's only a matter of time before Max is out altogether."

Now that he knew I wasn't a cop, he wasn't nearly as nervous about talking with me. As a matter of fact, he was putting on a phony air that belonged to neither the unsure man in stocking feet I talked to last time I was here, nor the strong male character he portrayed on the screen. I had no idea which of the three angles was real, or if there was a fourth and a fifth and maybe even a sixth Roger Francene."

"You say you and your sister are close?"

"*Were.* As children, we played in the same pictures together. Neither one of us was a star of course, but I think I learned by not being a star, by not having lines.

"Charlotte ruined herself by having tiny little speaking parts when she was ten or fifteen. She did those Republic Westerns, but she was never a star. She just considered herself a star. Child stars often get into movies when they grow up, but they never do learn to act."

"And now you're the star," I said.

He didn't pick up the sarcasm. Instead, he smiled as if I had just paid him a compliment.

"You seemed to have a great affection for Noni Light," I said, changing the subject.

"She was a sweet kid," he said, smiling nostalgically.

It took a long time for him to speak again, and it was he who broke the silence, but only to emphasize what he had already said.

"Yes, I did," he said. "I had a great affection for her."

"And?"

"She was a delightful girl. I liked her very much. After they passed her around the studio bosses and told her what she was expected to do, I . . ."

I waited.

". . . Well, I felt sorry for her. Just like I feel sorry for Lydia and some of the others. 'Screen test.' Ha!"

He rose and went over to the fireplace. In a dramatic posture, he rested his arm on the stones and stared into the cold hearth. Now, he thought he was John Barrymore in a silent film.

"Toby calls it a screen test," he said, and he turned away from the fireplace. "It's a pornographic film. He's got hundreds of them. He has no more intention of giving Lydia the part of Calamity Jane than he had of giving it to Noni. He'll have some young man, who also thinks he's going to be a star, make love to her in the most obscene ways, in Western costumes, as Romans or Greeks. He may even have them sing while they're doing it, and she won't get Belle Starr either."

His eyes were misting.

"That cruel son of a bitch – all those beautiful young girls."

I let him mourn for a moment. Then I asked him a lot more questions, but I learned nothing new. I had Pinch Scotch, no water, no ice, and we talked about the movies for a while. His butler kept coming into the room. Finally, Roger Francene went out and talked to him. He came back and explained, "The boy's jealous. He doesn't like to see me talk so long with another man."

After about another half-hour, Lydia hadn't shown up, and I went back to my office. Somebody had been there again, and the door had again been left unlocked. They were leaving me another message to get off the case.

CHAPTER 13

I called Kitty's number again and the answering service, still no news of her whereabouts. Then I went over to Warners on Sunset and asked for Miss Kazoo-voice by name. The guard called her office, and a blonde secretary came for me.

"Are you Detective Kane?" she said, sweetly. She was definitely not the woman I talked to on the phone.

"Kane's the name," I said, not wanting to overtly misrepresent myself.

"This way please," she said.

I loved walking behind her swinging hips. If this had been Morgan Studios, Max Morgan might have her in his pool of starlets. To Jack Warner's operation, she was a just an attractive secretary.

She was fine, but Miss Kazoo-voice looked just like she sounded: tall and narrow with padded shoulders and an upper row of white teeth that made her look like a horse. Her dark hair was intermingled with strands and patches of gray. I expected her to be wearing glasses but she wasn't. Her huge office was plain, with dozens of ledgers piled on the tables that lined the walls.

"What can I do for you, mmmmm?"

I reminded her that I was investigating the limousine that

had been stolen from the studio.

"I thought we gave your officer all the information you needed last week."

"You gave a lot," I said. I opened my old pocket note pad and flipped though the pages and stopped on something about the limousine.

"I'd like to go over it again," I said.

"Really? Mmmmm, how odd."

She touched her finger to her lips and twisted her brow. I was afraid she was going to ask to see a shield, but she didn't.

"Oh, well. Won't you sit down, mmmmm?"

None of the chairs in the room were padded, including her black swivel chair that must have been left over from before the war. This was an office for doing business, drab like mine, but a lot neater.

"Thanks," I said.

She opened a folder she had on her desk and began to paraphrase from what she saw.

"The limousine was out with the driver and one of our, shall we say, executives?" she said.

It was a disparaging comment, and I sensed she used the term "executive" very loosely.

"He was, mmmmm, looking for locations for a science fiction film we'll be doing soon," she said. "I understand the writer is one of the best of that field, Isaac Somebody-or-other?"

She raised her eyebrows waiting for me to acknowledge that I knew who she was talking about. When I didn't, she sighed at my ignorance and continued.

"Well, anyway, they left the limousine alongside Foothill Highway, a little north of San Fernando. When they came back, mmmmm, let me see. Yes. It was gone! We had to send someone out to pick them up."

"Who was the executive?"

"Mr . . . mmmmm . . . William Wells. We called him 'Billy.' He was new."

"You say 'was.' Is he dead?"

She laughed. "Oh, no, no. Of course not, but Mr. Jack Warner is not very patient with employees who lose our property – or get it stolen."

I liked the "our." It was as if she had a personal stake in it. "And the driver?"

"He's gone too."

"How long did he work for you?"

"Longer than Wells," she said.

"Can I have this guy Wells' address? And what about the other one, what do you have on him?"

"Let me get their files," she said and she went over to the middle of three wooden filing cabinets, pulled two files and carried them back to her desk. Sheepishly, she took a pair of glasses from the top drawer and fitted them carefully to her temples. Strangely enough, she looked better with the glasses than without them.

She opened one of the folders.

"Wells lives on Clarita Drive." She gave me the address, and she opened the other file. "And Teddy Cheeves, he lives . . . mmmmm . . . can you imagine that? He lives at the same address."

"Say the name again," I said, but I was sure I caught it.

"William Wells."

"No, the other one."

"Cheeves, Teddy," she said, and she spelled his last name. "It's probably really Theodore or Edward but we have him down as, mmmmm, yes, Teddy."

"Thank you very much," I said, and it cleared up the "Jeeves" business. I continued to ask questions as I scribbled down the names and the address. The address wasn't far from Kitty's place.

"Wells is bald, Cheeves is good looking. Right?" I said.

"Yes, I'd say that Cheeves is – well, he was always pushing to get a part in a film. He does have a certain, shall we say, 'animal charm'?" She laughed and continued. "The one time they gave him something as an extra, he stared straight at the camera until the director chased him off the set. He was a very good driver though, mmmmm, very good."

Her last "mmmmm" seemed to be an editorial comment of some sort, and she smiled as if it were a private joke. This was Hollywood. Maybe even Miss Kazoo worked with a casting couch.

"Thank you very much," I said, and I stood.

"I'm going to have to get someone to walk you back to the –"

I slammed the door over the end of her sentence, and I trotted toward through the front gate and across to the parking lot. The guard shouted after me, but I ran toward my car and put my key in the lock. I had the address now and those bastards –

"Kane!" I was startled by the voice of Kansas Michaels in the car beside me. "Leave you car. Come with me," he said.

"But I –"

"It's important," he said.

Oh, God, Kitty! With that look on his face, I thought the worst, and I slid quickly into the front seat with him. I had barely closed the door when he pulled off the lot, and headed west.

"What is it?" I said.

"I want you to look at something," he said. We drove another quarter mile, then he asked: "Have you heard from Kitty?"

"No," I said, and I felt a tightness in my chest. Has something happened to her?"

He didn't reply.

"Answer me, God damn you!"

"It might be nothing," he said.

"What do you mean, 'It might be nothing'?"

"Just be calm," he said.

I tried to hold on as he sped westward, but in a very few seconds, I demanded an answer, "You son of a bitch, you'd better tell me!"

Kansas sighed and looked over at me. Then he looked back at the road. I could tell he was thinking about how to word it, so I didn't push. After a while, he sighed. "We got a body. Could be her."

"Kitty?" I said. My chest squeezed even tighter.

He nodded, but he kept his eyes on the road in front of him.

The tears were trying to push from under my eyelids and I began to tremble. "If anything's happened to her, I'll get them," I said.

"Who?" said Kansas.

I didn't want to tell him about Wells and Cheeves or about the fake Charlotte Randolph. If he went after them, he'd take them alive. If I found out they killed Kitty, I'd save California the gas.

We came into Venice with the sun touching the ocean at almost the same spot where I made love to Kitty just a few days ago. He slowed for traffic lights, easing through the ones that were red. The sun was all but gone by the time he stopped the car.

There was a crowd gathered near the water's edge. About a half dozen uniformed cops encircled a small area, and I became more frightened as I approached. When I saw the dark hair fanned out over the sand, I became nauseous, but I held everything down. Except for the head, she was covered with a blanket. She must have been naked when they found her.

I closed my eyes as I stood over her, holding back whatever was in my stomach. Finally, I looked down. She had the high cheekbones, the slender face. *Oh God,* I thought. Tears were working under my eyelids.

Without thinking, I fell to my knees beside the body. Kitty and I were friends since just after the war. We understood each other like no one else understood us. What we had wasn't love, we refused to call it that. It was a kind of mutual respect and tolerance for each other's faults. I missed her the last few days and nights, and I worried about her. My greatest fear was that it would come to this.

I looked down at her, my vision blurred with tears that had still not yet spilled over my cheeks. I lost my mother when I was ten. The cheerleader I wanted to marry before leaving for the war was killed in an automobile accident, and now . . .

"Kitty," I whispered, and I continued to stare.

"Washed up about an hour ago," said one of the uniformed cops. "Shark took a couple of pieces out of her."

"Shut up!" Kansas snapped.

In that strange sickness of people who lose loved ones, I drew closer, looking at her face, that beautiful face.

Suddenly, I backed away and went upright on my knees. I frowned and twisted my head for a better angle. She was not only made up, she was painted, giving the impression of high cheekbones that weren't really there, giving the impression of dark lashes that weren't there either. Everything had been done to give the impression that this was Kitty, but . . .

"It's not her," I said.

"Get hold of yourself," said Kansas.

"It's not her," I said again.

"Come on, Kane. Settle down. You gotta get through it."

"I'm telling you it's *not* her. Somebody went to a hell of a lot of trouble to make it look like her, but that is not Kitty!"

"Are you sure?" said Kansas. He twisted his head to get a closer look.

Angry, I pulled back the blanket and a collective "Ooooo" went up from the crowd. The breasts were too large, and there was no California shaped birth mark on the left one. I covered her over and I stood.

"That is *not* her," I growled, pointing at the body. I looked at Kansas. "Get me back to my car."

On the way back to the Warner parking lot, I explained to him that Kitty was missing for the last couple of days, but I didn't tell him what Lydia Lane told me about Toby Wentworth's party, nor did I tell him about Wells and Cheeves.

I'd take care of them myself.

I intended to go straight to their Clarita Drive address and see what I could find out, but I thought about Lester Randolph and his missing boat. When Kansas let me off at my car, I drove back to the marina and found that Lester's boat was tied up at the pier. Without sneaking or asking anybody's permission, I climbed on board.

"Randolph!" I called, but there was no answer.

"Randolph!" I yelled again, banging on the door.

No one was there. I jimmied the lock into the cabin, but I found nothing that could help me. I walked down to the gate and asked the big guy in jeans and t-shirt how long the boat had been in port.

"What's it to you, Mac?"

"I'm investigating a murder," I said.

"Sorry," he said. He got very nervous and he shrugged. "Couple of hours I guess."

"Are you sure?" I said.

"Hey, I don't watch who goes in and out. But that's what I think."

I thanked him and went back to my car. I was thinking about Wells and Cheeves again as I drove through Beverly Hills on Santa Monica Boulevard. They were the ones who had hassled me, they were the ones who had told me to lay off the case, and they were probably the ones who sent me the photos of Kitty. I was thinking about all of that when I heard the high-pitched neep-neep from the horn of a sports car. It wasn't unusual for the neighborhood, but whoever was doing it was doing it for my benefit, and I glanced in the rear-view mirror.

The nearest car I saw was a half block away, and it was too big to make that kind of high-pitched noise. I heard it again, and I glanced to my left to see the M.G. beside me.

"Kitty!" I shouted.

I hit the brake and pulled quickly to the curb at Beverly Boulevard. Kitty rolled her M.G. to a stop behind me. I jumped from the Ford, and she jumped from the M.G. I was ready to wrap my arms around her, to hug her, to kiss her, and to tell her how much I missed her, but my smile froze with the sharp crack of her palm across my cheek.

"You son of a bitch!" she said.

She tried to slap me again, but I grabbed her wrist.

"What the hell's the matter with you?"

She tried to hit me with the other hand and I grabbed that wrist too.

"Where were you Monday?" she said.

"Where were you all week?" I said.

"Where were you!"

"What are you talking about?"

"I saw you chasing that bitch, Gloria Hastings through

Encino," she said. "You were driving like a crazy man, and you were laughing."

"What are you talking about?" I said again, but I knew exactly what she was talking about.

She growled though clenched teeth. "And I know you went to her place in Malibu because I followed you."

"What?" I said.

"I don't mind you making love to other women, but I hate it when you enjoy it so much."

"I'm working on a case," I said.

"You're always working on a case, and there's always a woman or two involved!"

"It's what I do for a living," I said, trying to sound reasonable.

"Bull shit! You don't have to like it so much."

"Kitty, I was worried about you."

"What difference does it make?"

"They said you were out of town. I thought something was wrong."

"Something was wrong, all right," she said. "*You* were wrong."

She broke into tears and her body went limp. I released her wrists, grabbed her upper arms and supported her weight.

"I don't like it when you go with other women," she said, sobbing. She pushed her head against my chest and I held her there.

"I can't help it," I said.

"I know, and neither can I," she said, her words muffled in my new seersucker jacket. "Take me to your place. Please?"

"I missed you so much," I said, and I kissed her long and hard.

"Hey, you two. You gonna move those cars?" said a Beverly Hills cop. He was off his motor cycle and carrying his book of tickets.

"Yes, sir!" I said, and he let us go on the tickets.

As soon as we were out of Beverly Hills, Kitty sped around me, and I chased her all the way to the lot behind my building. The first time we made love was on the floor in my living room. The second time was on the table in the kitchen. Finally, we went into the bedroom to relax.

"You're still working on that Noni Light case, aren't you?" she said, leaning back against the pillows.

"Yeah," I said. I wanted to tell her about the body on the beach, but I was afraid it would frighten her.

"Why are you still working on that one?"

"We've been through this before," I said.

"Did you love her?"

"Who?"

"Noni Light?"

"Kitty, what the hell's the matter with you. You know I don't fall in love."

"I sure do," she said.

She crossed her arms, not under her breasts, but over them with the California birthmark peeking out from under her wrist. Her head was turned only partially in my direction, and she was looking at me from the corners of her dark eyes.

It was as if she were trying to hide from me.

"We made that agreement. Right?" I said.

"Right," she said.

Her eyes filled with tears. Then suddenly, she wrapped her arms around me and pressed her naked body against mine.

"I missed you," I said.

I kissed the salty wetness of her eyes. I kissed her nose, her cheeks, her lips. The kiss was soft at first, flesh against flesh, but gradually our lips parted, and we drew on each other's souls. She rolled over on top of me and pushed the sheet down my body.

"Don't you ever tell me again that you missed me," she said, lying on top of me and holding me for a long moment. "Don't you dare tell me that!"

CHAPTER 14

In spite of the fact that Kitty was in my arms, I had trouble sleeping. I kept thinking about her on the boat with Lester Randolph and about the body that washed up on the beach. It could have been her, I kept thinking. Even when I awoke in the morning, "It could have been her," were the words I whispered to myself.

I slapped the alarm off and put my arms around her. I wanted to tell her I missed her, but I didn't want to start that discussion all over again. Later, with both of us wrapped in robes, we sat at my kitchen table drinking coffee and sharing a half-dozen glazed donuts. I decided to tell her the story Lydia Lane had told me about Sunday night and Monday morning.

"And what about you Monday afternoon?"

I said nothing. In that respect she was right, but she didn't have to worry about my safety. After I didn't reply, she spoke again. "You want me to verify that I spent Sunday night on his boat?" she said.

"No. I just want you to verify you weren't on his boat the last couple of days," I said. I wanted to know that because of the body.

"I wasn't on his boat the last couple of days," she said in a singsong. I couldn't tell if she was lying so that I'd know she was lying, or if she was so insulted by the question that she said it that way to irritate me.

Except for the fact that the body on the beach had been painted to look like her, she had a right to be insulted. I told her about the two hoods who didn't want me to investigate the Noni Light murder.

"They're blackmailing me," I said.

I went into the living room for the manila envelope, carried it back into the kitchen, and tossed it to the porcelain surface of the table.

"Take a look."

She glanced at the envelope and looked up at me, wondering what it was all about, but maybe fearing the answer.

"They were serious," I said. I handed her the note. Then I pushed the envelope across the table to her. I lit a Camel and I waited.

"What's this?" she said, as she absently unwound the string and opened the flap. There was a sick expression on her face, as if she might know already.

"Before you look at it, I want you to know that I don't care, except that it affects your safety."

Her breasts heaved and her fingers went inside the envelope. She hesitated before drawing out the photos.

"I don't think I want to see this," she said.

"It's important," I said. "I need to know the circumstance, because I'm afraid for you."

The look on her face was no longer fear, but anger. She looked down at the photo that showed her with her eyes open, her legs and arms spread.

"How much do you think you can get for these?" she said, sarcastically.

"The men who left them in my office are not selling, and they were not kidding. They want me off the Noni Light case."

"Then get off the case," she said in an off-handed way.

"You don't mean that?"

"Of course I mean it. You think I want this crap spread all over Hollywood? I've got a reputation, you know. This makes me look like a lush who can't hold her booze. Who wants to be seen with somebody like that?"

"Kitty. They've killed two women and . . ."

"Two?"

I hadn't intended to tell her about the one that was painted to look like her, but I had to let that out now.

"Yes," I said. "A woman washed up on the beach in Venice. She was shot with a .38, and I'll bet dollars to dimes it's the same .38 that killed Noni Light."

"Are you waiting till they kill me before you get off the case?" she said. She was trying to look tough, but her fingers were trembling.

"I just want to make damn sure they don't kill you," I said.

She spread all six photos on the porcelain and let out a single, "Huh." It was supposed to be a laugh, but it didn't come out that way. She let out another "huh" and another and another, until her body was quaking. She lowered her face to her hands and all the "huh's" ran together in hysterical sobs.

"I didn't spend all that time on the boat with him," she said. "I swear I didn't."

"I believe you," I said, but I wasn't sure.

I waited a long while before I asked her about the photos again. She shuffled through them several times. She looked sicker and sicker. Finally she stopped shuffling and stared at the awful one for a long time.

"They could have been taken anytime in the last couple of days," she said. "I was so damned out of it."

"What happened?"

"It was something they slipped me."

"You're a big girl. You know what's going on. How could that happen to you?"

She looked at me sharply, but decided against reacting in kind. "It can happen to anybody. Why should I be different?"

"I thought you were too smart for that."

"Look," she said, with an edge of bitterness. "When a girl goes out on a fare, she may have a couple of drinks, she gets a little tipsy, she might smoke something. You don't even think about what it is or how it will affect you. Before you know it, a couple of guys are dragging you into the bedroom and taking turns punching your card. You don't see cameras. You don't remember anything until a couple of days later when somebody you know pulls out a big brown envelope and shows you the pictures. Then you remember flash bulbs. You know you've done something stupid, but there's not a damn thing you can do to take it back. You just get on with your life, like always, and hope like hell you still have your friends."

I didn't say anything. I knew what Kitty did for a living. I didn't understand it, but I don't understand why I do some of the things I do either. I don't even understand why I'm a private eye – except that I do it very well and it pays good money.

"You want to call it quits with us? Is that it?" she said. "You want to stop being friends, that's fine with me. I don't screw up very often, but when I do, it's a dilly."

She turned the photos face down on the kitchen table and gathered them in like the next dealer dragging in his losing hand. The left side of her upper lip was quivering as she held back tears. She slipped the photos carefully back into the manila envelope, wound up the string and slid the whole package across the table at me.

"Something to remember me by," she said, with a sick smile.

"We're still friends," I said.

"Sure we are," she said, standing.

I looked at her, puzzled.

"Can't you get off the case?" she pleaded. "Can't you just let Kansas do his own God-damned job?"

"Why do you want me off?"

She took a deep breath and closed her eyes tightly over her tears. Then she spoke, "I saw the girl on the beach too," she said. She didn't open her eyes but tears were squeezing through, hanging on her long lashes.

"Somebody went to a hell of a lot of trouble to make her look like me."

"Let's get you out of town for a few days."

"What good would it do?"

"You'll be safe," I said.

"Nobody's ever safe in my profession."

I stood with her and put my arms around her. "I'll protect you."

"Sure you will."

"Let me take you to my place up the coast."

"I don't know," she said, but she let me hold her for a long time.

After about twenty minutes, she rustled out of my arms and sat up on the bed. "Can I use your phone?"

"Sure."

She called into her agency and her answering service, and said she'd be unavailable for still a few more days. She told me she would do what I asked, and we made love again.

On our way to my place near Carpinteria, she explained what happened the last couple of days: Toby Wentworth was giving her the star pitch, and she was falling for it like teen-ager from Cincinatti.

"He took the pictures?"

"I don't think so," she said. "After he got what he wanted, he was finished. Somebody else got me."

"At his place?"

"I don't think so, but I don't know. It was someplace in the hills. That's the best I can come up with. Whatever it was, they had me on some strong stuff."

We stopped off at the grocery store and got enough food for her to stay a week. All she'd have to go out for was milk and bread, and the grocery store was within walking distance.

When I got back to Hollywood the next morning, the headline on the Hearst paper screamed out from the sidewalk in front of Barney's news stand: "ANOTHER MORGAN STARLET MURDERED."

I got out of my Ford, dropped a nickel on the stack, and picked up the paper.

"Been goin' on all morning, Mr. Kane. Everybody's talkin' about it."

Barney, a pug nose ex-featherweight, was behind the newsstand. He was about fifty, from someplace in the East, Philadelphia, I think. He spoke with a nasal twang that was almost Cockney English. Part of it, I thought, had to do with his having been a boxer. The rest was accent.

"Makes you kind of nervous, huh? Don't dat look like Miss Kitty?"

I unfolded the paper and looked at the studio photo in the lower right hand corner of the front page. Barney was right. Jenny James, looked a hell of a lot like Kitty even with blonde hair and without the paint, and it made me very nervous.

"Does look a little like her," I said, trying to make it unimportant.

Sitting in my car, I read the whole article. When I arrived at my office, it was unlocked again. Whoever was doing it was trying to warn me. At first glance, nothing appeared to be disturbed, but when I looked more closely, I could see that things were moved subtly, as if they were trying to put things back exactly as they found them, but it didn't track with leaving the door unlocked. They were doing it too often.

They couldn't be that stupid. Eventually, they had to get caught – or maybe they were just delivering a message that I was too stubborn to get.

I parked my gray Ford along the white wall of Toby Wentworth's house, hit the intercom button, and told the butler who I was.

"Wait a minute," said the butler gruffly.

In a few seconds he came back to the intercom and told me to come up the walk. The huge man opened the front door without a greeting and he led me on the white tour through the house. I wasn't even blinded by the sunlight as led me out the French doors at the rear of the house and down the wide, marble stairs to the pool.

As expected, everything at the pool was white, including the umbrellas and the tables under them. Toby Wentworth was in the sun, leaning back on a white chaise, wearing – surprise of surprises – a pair of white bathing trunks. His previously white skin was a little red from the sun but he fixed some of that with a white cream on his nose.

"It's no wonder you're trying to get to the bottom of his thing about Noni Light, she was a beautiful young lady," he said.

Bull shit, I thought and I knew his next words would be about the Calamity Jane picture.

"She would've gotten such good exposure in *Jane*. She

could have been a star eventually, you know."

It was more bull shit, but I smiled. A few days ago, he was telling me there had been no chance for Noni. He was, no doubt, about to release his current story to the press and he was trying it out on me.

"How are you coming with the casting. Who's in line?" I said it like a friend who had dropped in for a chat. But this man was anything but a friend.

"Everybody's getting in line," he said. "It's like *Gone With the Wind*. You know, everybody wanted to play Scarlett. Now, everybody wants to play Jane."

Sure, I thought, but everybody in Hollywood knew about Scarlett O'Hara. I never even heard of *Jane* or the Calamity Jane picture until I started to work on this case.

"I've got my eye on someone," he said. "A newcomer."

"Did you ever think about Jenny James? The girl they found washed up on the beach in Venice yesterday?"

He pushed his lips together and tilted his head to the side. While I waited, I lit up a Camel.

"I considered her only briefly," he said. Then he laughed. "Can you imagine me having Jenny James play Jane? 'Jenny James as Jane.' '*Jane*, with Jenny James.' It would be the joke of the industry. They'd never let me up. Max Morgan would never stand for it, and Louie Mayer would gloat about me leaving Metro. Andrea Anderson would laugh the studio into bankruptcy. We're in enough trouble already."

"I understand Max Morgan is on the way out?"

He shrugged. "Max is still in charge. Dick Wrenking only thinks he's running things," he said. Apparently, nobody but Max Morgan and Dick Wrenking knew the real story.

"What do they have to say about *Jane*?"

"They don't have much to say," he said, raising one eyebrow over the edge of his white rimmed sunglasses. "I told them I wouldn't do the picture unless they let me take care of the casting myself."

"Do you have absolutely free reign with the studio's starlets?" I asked the question somewhat bitterly, and he didn't pick that up.

"I can choose absolutely anyone I want for this. In or out of the studio, out of the industry, if I choose," he said. He was bragging, but it suddenly hit him. "Why are you asking all these questions?"

"Just trying to tie some things in with the Noni Light case," I said, but I was getting impatient. "Do you know a woman by the name of Kitty Chaney?"

His face froze over for just a moment, and he shifted quickly to an expression of bewilderment. He was trying to use some of his old acting skills.

I took a drag on my Camel and waited.

Finally, his eyes popped wide as if he made a discovery. "Yes, yes. I remember now, a young lady named Kitty something-or-other, a model for a couple of the local department stores. I could screen test her. Do you know her?"

"I've met her," I said. I flicked the gray at the end of my Camel into the white ashtray on the table beside him.

He watched my hand, as if it were an insect and he gave an involuntary snarl. "I've been meaning to contact her agency. She is a model, but I'm sure they'd be happy to take a fee from Morgan."

If I didn't know he was a lying son of a bitch out to get every woman he wanted into his bed, I would have been excited for Kitty, and I wouldn't have noticed the insincerity behind it.

"Tell me something, Detective Kane," he said. "Just why do you keep coming to see me? I haven't given you the first clue that will help you find Noni Light's killer."

I took another drag on my Camel. "You were one of the

last people to see her alive, and you've given me more clues than you can imagine."

"Really?" he said, incredulous.

"When's the last time you saw Jenny James?"

"Months," he said, looking directly at me.

"Tell me about your little party Sunday night?"

"Jenny was not there," he said firmly, "and I'm a bit puzzled. Is the, uh, Los Angeles Police Department following me, Detective Kane?"

"Not that I know about." I tapped my Camel into the ashtray again, and he looked distastefully at the ashes. Apparently the white ashtrays were never intended to be used.

"Walter!" he called. Then he turned to me. "Am I suspect?"

"At this point, everyone's a suspect. You're just one of many."

Walter stepped from between one set of the French doors and glided down the marble stairs like a giant on a cloud.

"Perhaps I shouldn't say anything else. For fear that I'll get myself into some kind of trouble." he said, and Walter arrived poolside. "Would you empty that disgusting thing?"

"Yes, sir," said Walter. He took the ash tray and climbed the wide marble stairs leaving no place for me to put my ashes.

"Can you tell me a little more about that party Sunday night?"

"It's none of your business," he said, the words buzzing at me.

"I understand if the L.A.P.D. had come to your party, you'd be looking for a new job. You know, the morals clause and all that."

He took a deep breath. His face, already red from the sun, was now even redder. "Where did you hear about my party?"

"A little bird told me."

"What's the little bird's name?" he growled.

"How many little birds did you have at your party?" I asked with mock sweetness, as if I were talking to a child.

"You know, what's your name . . . Kane? Well Kane, I don't like it when somebody comes to my place and wants to ask me all about my business. I like it even less when they want to *tell* me about my business. I've got connections in Los Angeles who will get you off me just as fast as you got on me. So don't think that just because you've got a badge that you can push me around."

I wondered how he'd react if he knew I didn't have a badge.

"What else do you want to ask me?" he said. "Then I want you to get the hell out of here."

"Who's going to play the lead in *Jane*?" I asked again, just to antagonize him.

He took a deep breath. Then he let the words pour out in anger. "When the star and her agent find out, then the world will find out – but not before. I am damn sure not going to give that scoop to the Los Angeles Police Department. And what the hell does it have to do with your murder investigation?"

I raised my eyebrows. I was down to the butt of my Camel.

"You cops are a nuisance, do you know that? First you, then that other one, Texas or whatever-the-hell his name is. Now it's you again. When do I have to stop answering questions?"

"You talk to a lawyer yet?"

"What the hell do I need a lawyer for? I'm not hiding anything. I think I've answered as many questions as I'm going to answer in one day – and I will talk to my contacts at City Hall. Now, if you don't mind, I want to get a little more of this sun before it's too late."

"How many girls did you have at your party?"

"Walter?" he shouted, rising from his chaise. The veins in his neck were so engorged, I thought he might burst an artery.

In seconds, the giant of a butler stepped from between a set of the French doors and hurried smoothly down the stairs toward us.

"Detective Kane is just leaving," said Wentworth. "Won't you see that he gets safely to his car?"

"Yes, Mr. Wentworth," said Walter. His voice was as deep as if it had come from the bottom of a well. "This way please, Detective Kane."

Were I real cop, I could have threatened them now, and I might get away with it. But my credentials were weak. All I had was my private investigator's license, and in the present situation, it was not only useless but it might well be at risk. I sighed, shrugged, and snapped the butt of my Camel into the clean water of the pool.

I smirked at Wentworth. Then I turned, walked around the pool and climbed the white marble stairs, retracing my steps through the white house and through the yard to my gray Ford.

The next time I tried to see Toby Wentworth, I was pretty sure I wouldn't get in by invitation. When I got back to my office, it was locked, just as I left it. I called Kitty at my place in Carpenteria and talked to her for about half an hour. She assured me that as far as she knew Jenny James had not been at Toby Wentworth's party. I slept alone, thinking about Kitty and about the body of Jenny James. In the morning I went to the Morgan Studios to talk to Lester Randolph. After a lot of red tape, a gum-popping, studio guide led me back to Lester's office.

She was a freckle-faced redhead. She was not the stuff stars are made of – unless your name is Judy Garland or June Allyson.

CHAPTER 15

I was surprised that Lester Randolph's office was only slightly more elaborate than that of Miss Kazoo-voice over at Warners. The walls were beige, the desk was mahogany and the chair behind it was padded in brown leather. There was an adjacent room, probably a bath. On his desk was a stack of scripts, one of which had a pencil stuck in the middle.

"We meet at last," Lester Randolph said, standing and offering his hand.

"Pardon?" I said.

"Everybody's told me about you," he said. "You're the policeman who's running around trying to pin somebody with the Noni Light murder."

His wry smile turned sarcastic, and he motioned for me to sit in the sofa against the wall opposite his desk.

"I'm not trying to pin it on anybody," I said. "I'm trying to find out who did it."

Randolph was good looking in the traditional tall and handsome sense, but he was anything but dark. His hair was blond, almost white. His eyes were a baby blue, and his complexion was more gold than dark. His features had a sharp, chisel cut, like those of a Greek or Roman statue. His role on the screen was the tough guy. In that respect, he wasn't much different from Roger Francene, except that his toughness was manufactured, now with the arrogance of a smirk.

"Am I one of your suspects?" he said. He thought he was being disarming, but I came back with a verbal punch in the gut.

"Definitely," I said.

His eyes opened wide under his bushy brows. "Very frank of you," he said.

"There are some things that point to you," I said, trying break his cockiness, and before he asked what those things were, I told him I knew about his meetings with Noni.

"If that's the case, I can give you the names of a half dozen other people who were with her," he said.

"I've got several of my own," I said, lighting up a Camel.

"You want to hear the names?" he said.

"Why not?" I said.

He gave me five names, which included Roger Francene, Toby Wentworth, Clark Gable, and three others I considered as only outside possibilities.

"I suspect a woman too," I said. "She tried to pass herself off as your wife."

His golden tan drained, and he sat back in his chair, stunned.

"You know her?" I said.

"I know *of* her," he said. "I haven't heard about her in a few years, but I *definitely* know *of* her."

"What exactly does that mean: you know 'of her'?"

He looked down at his desk and brought his hand to his lips. Finally, he looked over at me.

"What do *you* know about her?" he said.

"She hired a private detective to follow you," I said.

"What?"

"The private detective on the case thinks she was trying to break up your marriage. She claimed to be your wife, and she wanted him to mail the report to your house."

"Oh, my God!" he said, and his body went limp. "Did he do it?"

"We don't think so," I said. I was telling the literal truth, but what he really wanted to know was if Charlotte had seen the report. She had, of course, but I wouldn't tell him that, nor would I let him know that I was the private detective I referred to. He still thought of me as a cop.

"What did he find out about me?" said Randolph.

"That you're seeing a couple of starlets. One of them was Noni Light, the little girl who got murdered last week."

"If you know all this, why haven't you talked to me before?"

"I was trying to give it the old 'give a man enough rope and he'll hang himself' routine."

"I haven't hanged myself because I didn't have anything to do with it," he said.

"Let's try again," I said. I inhaled and nodded. "Before we got off the track, I asked what you know about this woman who tries to pass herself off as your wife."

"Actually, I know very little."

"But what do you know?"

There was a long pause as he thought about it. Finally, he spoke: "Somebody delivered some pictures of her. Then they called me back and tried to blackmail us."

He was staring at the far corner of his desk. The words came out slowly and cautiously, as if he were telling a story he never told before, and he wanted to get the details just right. It could be that it happened exactly that way, but that was also the way a lot of people told a well-prepared lie.

"It was about three years ago," he said. "We were doing a World War II picture on one of the sound stages. It was late in a long day. I went back to my dressing room and there was a manila envelope on my makeup chair. I don't need much makeup, so I do my own. Actually, I sat on the damn thing before I realized it was there."

Lester Randolph smiled, a bit embarrassed. He either didn't want to tell the story, or he was pretending he didn't want to. I had to be careful because he was a better actor than Toby Wentworth. He paused for a long time. Then he started to talk again.

"I thought somebody left some fan photos for me sign, so I just threw them on the makeup table." He forced a chuckle. "Have you ever seen an actor with a face full of cold cream? He looks exactly like an actress, Mr. Kane."

I smiled politely.

"I was wiping the cold cream off, but I couldn't keep my eyes off that envelope. Something about it was significant. I got impatient. I wiped my hands and untied the envelope. When I slid out the photos, I knew they weren't for me to sign."

His eyes dropped from the wall, and he looked straight at me. "In spite of what I've done, I think our marriage has been good."

I waited.

"At first glance, I thought the photos were of Charlotte, and I got sick. She was making love to some young stud, an actor, I thought at first. Then I realized it wasn't an actor at all, just a good looking nobody who probably wanted to be an actor, and thought that posing for pornographic photos was the way to go about it."

He stopped talking again. Stared at his desk for a moment.

"Do you now what it's like to see photos of the woman you love with —" There was a pause and I expected more, but it never came.

"I thought you said it wasn't her," I said, but I also thought of the photos of Kitty that somebody had dropped on me.

"It wasn't her," Randolph said, "but I thought it was. Even

thinking about it now, I feel sick inside. She didn't just look just a little like Charlotte. She looked a hell of a lot like Charlotte."

"How did you know it wasn't her?"

"It's very personal," he said.

"What do you mean?"

"I can't tell you, but you can trust me. It's personal."

I nodded. "You still have the photos?"

"It's . . . they're personal."

"You told me they're not your wife."

"They're not her, but it's almost the same thing. They look so much like her that –"

"I'd like to see them."

He looked hard at me but his cheeks were pink. Then he sighed and pulled open one of the bottom drawers of his desk. He rummaged past a stack of folders and came up with a manila envelope. It had been untied so often, the string was gone. The envelope had a red border, like the one they used to send me Kitty's photos. Lester slid it across the blotter to me.

I pulled back the flap and slid three photos from inside. I raised my eyebrows. They looked damned good, I thought. They were professional and well posed.

"It's not her," he said.

It sure did look like Charlotte, I thought, but it looked even more like the woman who had hired me to follow Lester.

He took a deep breath as I fingered through the photos. The woman was lying on her back, one knee up and covering her crotch. Her lover was beside her, with his hand between her legs. She had fuller breasts than Charlotte and a bit more meat on her body, but the man in the photo was Teddy Cheeves, his mouth open breathlessly. The woman wore a smile that women reserve not for the camera but for the satisfaction of carnal pleasure.

In the second photo, the woman was engaged in active sex, while Cheeves was passive but clearly enjoying what was being done to him. I must have stared a moment too long, because Lester huffed his impatience. I slid to the third photo. It was a strange one: the Charlotte Randolph imposter was in a pink night gown, kneeling up and facing the camera in a pose made famous by Rita Hayworth.

"That's enough!" he snapped, and he reached for the photos.

I didn't give them to him immediately. Instead, I shuffled to the first photo. The woman was clearly enjoying being touched, but she was looking cynically at the camera and touching the nipple of her own left breast. The disk around it was the size of a silver dollar.

"Not her, huh?" I said.

"No," he said.

"Can I take these?"

"What for?"

Evidence? A clue? No, the fact was that these pictures had given me a renewed interest in Charlotte Randolph. It had taken a while for her to come up with the right time and the right place, but when she did, I had turned her down. I was anxious to compare the woman I saw in these photos with what I would see when I got an intimate close-up of the real thing.

"Never mind," I said, "but don't let anything happen to them."

"I've had them for three years. I won't let anything happen to them now."

"Did you recognize the guy?"

"Yeah, he was right here on the Morgan lot, trying to break into the movies. I guess he figured dirty pictures and blackmail was a good way to do it. It cost him his job and his chance."

"You didn't call the police?"

"No. Not worth the aggravation, and it would definitely

bring too much newsprint."

"Ever find out who the woman was?"

"No. This guy said he had no idea how to reach her, but he was going back to Chicago. Now you tell me they're at it again?"

"Seems that way. Did they contact you yet?"

"No, but it won't work. Another guy, another woman, another studio, maybe. But they're wrong again. With us it won't work."

"What did they want the first time?"

"Money for her. Some good parts for him. I got him fired, but I told him if those pictures got into the wrong hands, I'd make sure he went to jail. He's got to be crazy."

"And that was it? Nothing more? No follow up? No threats a couple of years later?"

"That was it, except . . ." Lester took a deep breath. "She'd call me from time to time. Offer to see me for a thousand dollars. 'Find out what a really lousy piece of ass your wife is,' she said."

"You never did anything?"

"I thought about it. I thought about it a lot, but no, I never did anything. The way I figured it, that would be asking for trouble. If she were blackmailing me with photos of her and some idiot, she'd blackmail me even worse with whatever *we* did."

I studied him, watched the way he fidgeted, looked where his eyes went. There was a damn good chance he was telling the truth, but I couldn't be sure. I let a long pause hang between us. Then I went off on a different line of thought.

"You know a woman by the name of Kitty Chaney?"

"Never heard of her."

"Lydia Lane?"

"She's one of our contract players."

"Ever see them both together?"

There was a slight tinge of pink at his cheeks. "I told you I never heard of the first one."

"Who were you with on your boat Sunday night?"

The pink was still in his cheeks, but his ears were now scarlet. I waited.

"I was with Lydia and another woman."

"Describe her?"

He described Kitty perfectly. He thought it took him off the hook. Maybe he didn't know her name, but he knew who I was talking about."

"Where did you go when you left the marina?"

"How do you know I left the marina?"

"I checked with the swallows at Capistrano," I said.

He didn't answer immediately. Finally, he shrugged. "I went to Catalina. I always go to Catalina."

"Alone?"

"Yes," he said.

"Where do you stay?"

"Just off the beach. I drink a little, think a little. Hell, I might even try to catch a fish or two."

"Alone?"

"I . . ."

"Who with?"

"That other girl. The one whose name I don't know."

Kitty told me she hadn't been with him.

"How about Jenny James," I said. "You never heard of her either?"

"I heard of her, but I never knew her. Look, I didn't have anything to do with her. She was a starlet here. She washed up on the beach yesterday. I swear, I had nothing to do with her."

"She washed up about the same time you were docking your boat."

"How do you know what time I docked the boat?"

"We checked."

"I know it sounds strange but, I swear, I had nothing to do with Jenny James. Look, I'll try to get in touch with the woman who was with me."

"Why don't you give me her phone number," I said.

"She wouldn't like cops having her number," he said.

I nodded. If Kitty were on the boat with him, there was no way he could have killed Jenny James, unless . . . I didn't even want to think about that. I had most of what I needed from him and I was damned uncomfortable with it. I stood and started for the door.

"There's one more thing," Lester said.

"Yeah?"

"The room in those pictures – it's one of the rooms at Toby Wentworth's place."

"Did you ask him about it?" I said.

"He denied he knew anything about the pictures or the woman. I told him they looked like my wife, and he just raised his nose, the bastard."

"And what did you say?"

Lester was silent.

"Well?" I said.

"I didn't say anything," said Lester. "The way Hollywood's going these days, with television coming in, I might have to work for him some day."

"Thanks," I said.

Lester Randolph was a real hero. A man of principle. Everybody in Hollywood had principles. Sure.

CHAPTER 16

I didn't want to go sneaking around Beverly Hills in broad daylight, especially since a gray Ford is not something that would go unnoticed in the neighborhood of Cadillacs and Lincolns and Packards. They'd also notice a man on foot in a seersucker suit – who might be detected carrying a .38 Special under his jacket. I called Charlotte from a phone booth on Wilshire Boulevard to ask if I could come over to see her.

"Oh, yes," she said, with an inflection that told me she recognized my voice and was glad to hear from me, but it also told me that she couldn't talk at that moment.

"Lester's at the studio," I said. "Are the children in school?"

"Yes."

"Is there someone else with you?"

"I'll send the maid down to Long Beach to pick it up," she said, her comment explaining why she couldn't talk.

"Does that mean you want me there?" I said.

"Of course," she said.

"Be there in fifteen minutes."

"That'll be fine," she said, and she hung up.

It was a glorious California day, warm but not hot. I lit up a Camel outside the phone booth and waited. Charlotte would again ask for photos of her husband with some other woman, but I was so wrapped up in trying to find out who killed Noni Light and Jenny James that I almost forgot that keeping my fee depended on getting those pictures – almost forgot, but not quite.

I thought about that several times while talking to Kitty. She was an obvious candidate, and it would be easy set up, but every time I thought about it, I realized I'd never asked her to do anything like that before and wasn't about to do it now. It was the kind of thing friends never asked friends to do – especially not the kind of friends we were.

Right now, Lydia and maybe Gloria Hastings were my only hopes of getting a photo of Lester with somebody, and I wasn't sure I could even pull that off. My best bet was to act like an old fashioned private dick: just sneak up on him when he was with one of his women and snap a picture or two. It's the ugly part of my business, but it's the part that keeps bread on the table and a little money in the bank.

I tossed my Camel to the sidewalk, smeared it out with my foot, and climbed into the Ford. I drove with my windows down, letting the warm breeze sweep past me. Nat King Cole was singing "Mona Lisa" on the radio, so I stayed in the car a little longer and drove a little farther. When the song ended, I doubled back to Palm Drive and took my Ford up to the front door of the un-walled Randolph hacienda. Like an invitation, the iron grate was unlatched and the front door was slightly ajar. I clinked open the iron grate and stepped into the house, pulling the huge door closed behind me.

"Hello?" I called, but there was no answer.

Her car was gone, but she said something about sending the maid for something or other. *How many maids owned a car?* I stood in the entryway and looked into the living room, but Charlotte was not there. I stepped down the hall and looked through open doors into the kitchen and the formal dining room. *God, the furniture was big*, I thought. I went back to the entryway and looked up the staircase: heavy, in dark wood contrasting with the stucco of the walls. White walls or not, the house was dark compared to the blazing white of Toby Wentworth's place.

I eased through the downstairs rooms, including a den, a pantry, and a viewing room. I looked out over the pool. There was no one there.

Finally, I went back to the entryway and climbed the stairs carefully, making as little noise as possible. When I reached the overhanging walkway, I carefully moved first to one end of the house and to the other. Most of the rooms were open: kid's bedrooms, guest bedrooms, a bedroom that obviously belonged to a man who hunted and fished, and two baths that opened near opposite ends of the hall.

Only one room was closed. I stood outside and listened, but I heard nothing. I tapped lightly, but there was still no answer. I tapped again and waited. Finally I touched the latch and pushed open the door. In the huge room was a lace-canopied four-poster bed and three other pieces of dark furniture. There was no one in the room but I heard running water in the adjacent bath.

"Hello," I called.

The door opened, and out stepped Charlotte Randolph, wrapped in that same gray, silk robe she wore the first morning I saw her. The sash hung loose but she held the whole thing closed with her arms crossed under her breasts.

She might have stepped from a shower, except that her hair was impeccable, twisted back the way she wore it at Moonset a couple of days ago.

"What took you so long," she said.

"Just cautious," I said.

"The maid won't be back for an hour," she said. "And once

Lester's at the studio, he never comes home."

It sounded like a lovely marriage, I thought, and I wondered why it had taken so long for her to realize he was running around on her.

"Do you have my pictures?" she said.

"No," I said.

"Oh?" she said, raising her eyebrows. "Then why are you here?" she said.

"Just came to touch bases," I said.

"Do you often come into a woman's bedroom just to touch bases?" She sucked in on her cheeks, laughing with her eyes.

"Sometimes," I said, smiling. "But only when I'm looking for the right time and the right place."

"This may be it," she said.

Her expression twisted to a sardonic, almost evil smile. When she uncrossed her arms, her robe fell open, and a ribbon of dark and light flesh showed down the middle of her body. I raised my eyebrows, and she stepped forward, stretching her arms toward me. The robe opened even farther, showing the under curve of her breasts, the mound of her pubis, the streaks of white where her bikini bathing suit had blocked the sun. Her nipples peeked past the lapels of her robe. That was why Lester knew it wasn't her in the photos, I thought. The woman in the photos had silver-dollar size moons around her nipples. Charlotte's moons were almost non-existent, but the nipples were hard and thick, like the tips of my little fingers.

"When are you going to get me the pictures?" she whispered, startling me. For a moment, I thought she was asking about the photos Lester had shown me. Then I remembered the ones I was supposed to take, but I stepped closer to her, slid my arms around her. Her breath was peppermint sweet as her lips lightly touched mine. There was just the barest hint of wet in the subtlety of her tongue. It was the kiss I'd been waiting for since the first minute I saw her.

"Do private detectives always wear jackets?" she said, helping me slip out of my coat.

"The better to hide their guns, my dear."

"That's not that gun I'm interested in."

She helped me out my shoulder holster, and we let it ease to the floor.

She slid her hand up my leg to the front of my trousers.

"Now that's a gun," she said.

I kissed her, softly. I had been waiting for the right time and the right place, and this was it. I raised my hand to her breast and touched my fingers lightly to her firmly erect nipple.

"Ooooo . . ." she said, and she kissed me so hard, so full and so rich that it took my breath away. My other hand slid under the silkiness of her robe to her buttocks. She danced me back to the four-poster bed and pulled me on top of her as we fell together under the canopy.

As we lay locked in a kiss and an embrace, she deftly unbuckled my belt, unbuttoned the top button of my trousers, lowered the zipper. Her nails slid over my hard buttocks as she pushed down my trousers and drew me upward.

"Now is definitely the right time and the right place," she said, guiding me, and I slipped easily into her.

"I've waited for so long, so long," she said, tears rolling over her cheeks.

I kissed her lightly, and as I made love to her I had the sense that she was a woman starved for love. In spite of her desperation, I treated her gently. It was only her kiss that was feverish; the rest of our movements were slow, almost resistant, and I sensed that to her what we were doing was more like love than sex, and I was pleased. For a moment, it made me think about Kitty, but I had to push it out of my mind.

As soon as I was comfortable with the slowness, she began

to thrust herself up at me. Then she went into a frenzy and began to cry out. She pulled her lips from mine and began to turn her head violently from side to side.

"That son of a bitch," she cried. Then she screamed Lester's name and wrapped her legs around me, her bare heels kicking into my legs and buttocks as if I were a horse refusing to respond.

"That dirty, rotten, son of a bitch!" she cried, riding up at me. "Yes! Yes! That son of a . . . son of a . . . son of a . . . Oh . . . oh . . . bitch, bitch, bitch!"

She let out a long sigh, bucked one more time and she was finished. It wasn't exactly the way I imagined it would be. I wanted there to be more. I wanted it to last longer.

But it was just fine.

After I smoked a cigarette, we made love again, this time less urgently, and I learned what I wanted to know without saying a word. In the brightness of her room, under the lace of the Spanish four-poster bed, I again determined there were definite similarities between Charlotte and the imposter in the photograph, but there were also differences of detail. The imposter was heavier, more buxom. The imposter wore pounds of makeup, and, as I had observed before, the imposter had huge moons around her nipples. I was comfortable with the comparison.

"I want those photograph's of Lester and *anybody*," she said, almost as a threat, as I slung my holster over my shoulder.

"I'll get them," I said.

"I don't care if you have to go out on that God-damned boat with him, I want them," she said, sounding very different from the woman I had just made love to.

"Did you find out anything more about this woman who looks like you?" I said.

"You're the one who's supposed to be looking into that."

"Right," I said, now embarrassed at my own question. She helped me into my jacket. I had waited for the right time and the right place, and it was worth it. Now, I had to get back to work.

"One for the road," she said. She kissed me softly and for a long time.

I didn't want to leave, but I had things to do, and the maid was due back shortly. I again had the feelings of guilt about Kitty creeping up on me. It was something Kitty and I had worked out over a long period of time, but I never quite stopped feeling guilty about it. Neither did Kitty.

And she was a call girl.

I ordered a ham-on-rye and a beer at Jocko's. While I waited, I called Kitty at my place at Carpenteria. There was no answer, but she was probably walking on the beach. After I finished eating, I called Kitty again. There was still no answer. She loved to walk the beach in the evening, I thought.

Then I called Lydia Lane.

"What do you want?" Lydia said abruptly, as if I was interrupting something.

"I know you spend a lot of time at Wentworth's place," I said. Then I tried to be casual. "Did you ever run into a woman who looks like Charlotte Randolph?"

There was a silence on the other end of the line.

"Well?" I said, after a few seconds.

"Maybe," she said.

"Somebody there with you?"

"Can you call me in about a half hour?"

"Are you all right?"

"I'll be fine," Lydia said, and she hung up.

That puzzled me, so I drove to her apartment hotel. I watched the front door of the building for an hour and saw nobody I knew either coming or going. Then I went to a phone booth and called her. The man at the desk told me there was no answer. From the same booth, I called Kitty again, and there was again no answer. She liked the beach, yes, but it wasn't like her to spend the whole day there.

She should have been home by now. She and Kansas were the only ones who knew about my place in Carpinteria, but I still panicked. I jumped into my Ford and I exceeded the speed limit all the way up the coast.

The lights were on in the front room of my cabin. By force of professional habit, I parked about a hundred yards away, and walked quietly along the road. I eased onto the porch and looked through the windows.

At first, I saw no one, but that was more out of fear than fact. After I got my emotions under control, I realized that Kitty was sitting, clearly alive, in my easy chair, reading *Forever Amber* for about the twentieth time.

I tapped lightly at the door. She looked up and squinted in my direction. Then she rose and came toward me. She put her ear to the door, somehow thinking that no one would see her through the glass.

"Who's there," she said.

"Kane," I said.

Her worried expression shifted to anger. She unbolted the door, yanked it open, and shouted, "Why the hell didn't you call me?"

"You didn't answer," I said, stepping inside.

Her eyes watered, and she wrapped her arms around me. She held me close, but for only a moment. Then she relaxed and pushed me away.

"I was worried about you," she said.

"No more than I was about you," I said. I closed the door and took her gently in my arms. It felt good just knowing she was safe.

I went to the small kitchen, grabbed two bottles of Golden Beer from the refrigerator, took two pilsner glasses from the cabinet, and carried them into the rustic living room. Whenever I stayed here, I always thought the same thing: it was like the setting for a Steinbeck novel. It was probably why I bought the place.

"I called you three times in the last two hours. You've never spend that much time on the beach. The seals usually scare you off."

"Worried I had a guy up here?" she said.

"You were missing for a couple of days, and that wasn't easy for me. Those guys threatened me. It was no fluke that the girl who washed up on the beach in Venice was painted to look like you."

"And that's all it is."

I tried to think of the right words so they wouldn't come out sounding stupid.

"Look," I said. "Sometimes it's tough for me to ask the question I really want to ask."

She sipped some of the beer and glared at me, "Ask."

I cleared my throat. "Well, you know . . . Did you spend all that time with Lester Randolph on his boat?"

Her lips pursed. Then they curled. "I told you I did not spent all that time on his boat – just Sunday night. Why do you keep asking."

"When did Lydia leave?"

Kitty sighed. "Do we have to go through all this?"

"If we want to find out who killed Noni Light we do."

She sighed and shook her head. "We don't care who killed Noni Light, only you do. But the other 'we', me and Lydia, left his boat early Monday morning. After that, I think he went out on the water."

"How do you know?"

Her cheeks flushed and she sighed. "I went down to the dock. He wasn't there," she said.

"Oh," I said.

"'Oh' is right," she said. "I went back there because he said he had a good fare for me."

"Was anybody else with you and Lydia?"

She raised her eyebrows. "What are you trying to do? Trap me? Why do you have to ask all this crap? You know what I do. It's what I get paid to do. We've talked about it dozens of times. I do what I do. You do what you do." She finished in a huff. Then she stepped forward and touched my face with her fingertips.

"This one's getting tough. I need to know if anybody else was on the boat with you and Lydia and Lester."

"Nobody!" She drained her glass and poured more beer.

"Could anybody else have gone on his boat?"

"Of course. I was gone for a couple of hours. Why don't you leave me alone about this?" she said, and she drained the beer she had just poured.

"This isn't just a snoop job for a divorce case anymore," I said. "We've got two murders."

"Kane, you know, your cases always seem to get mixed up in my life, and I don't like it. I don't mind talking to you about them, because it makes me feel useful, but I don't like being a suspect."

"Who said you were a suspect?" I asked hoarsely.

"Do you think I'm stupid?" she said. She went to the refrigerator and opened another bottle of the Golden. This time, she took a swig directly from the bottle. "You sound like Kansas interrogating a witness."

I waited before I asked the next question. "Did you ever meet Jenny James?"

"Yes," she snapped.

"Yes?"

"Yes," she said, impatiently. "She was a Morgan girl. You can put them in a bag, shake them up, and you couldn't tell them apart. Lydia, Jenny, Noni, the rest at Morgan, a dozen more over at MGM, and more scattered around the other studios. Bleached blondes, every one of them, and not one of them with talent."

I nodded. "How well did you know Jenny?"

"Not well at all, but I knew her well enough to know she was not with us on Sunday, if that's your next question."

I sighed, uncomfortable about asking her anything since Lester said Kitty was on the boat with him the last few days.

"What kind of shape was Lester in when you left him?"

"The same shape he was in when he propositioned me and Lydia: drunk or drugged or both. He was totally out of it, I doubt that he remembers a damned thing that happened."

He said he remembered spending the last few days on the boat with her, but I wasn't going to challenge her with that. Kitty and Kansas were my only two friends. I was getting close to losing Kitty, but there were things I had to know.

"Was Jenny at Toby Wentworth's party?"

"She might've been there. There were so damn many people there."

"Now think of her as a brunette and tell me if she was there."

She looked confused, but I could see by the twist of her brow that she was trying to imagine Jenny as a brunette, maybe even trying to remember her disguised as Kitty herself.

"I don't think so." She said it firmly, but without conviction.

Her lips were pushed tightly together like an old woman's. Finally, she tipped the bottle upward and drained it.

"Would you mind taking me back to Los Angeles?" she said bitterly. "Maybe we can be friends again after this whole thing blows over."

"It's not safe for you in Los Angeles."

"And I'm not sure I want to stay here."

"I'm sorry. You know I didn't mean anything. It's just that —"

She stood, her arms crossed, waiting for an excuse, but I couldn't come up with one. Instead, I went for a reason: "I've got to find out who killed her."

She was still waiting.

"I talked to Lydia on the phone, but there was somebody with her, and she couldn't talk. She may know the woman who looks like Charlotte Randolph. When I called her back, there was no answer."

"You didn't go in? You didn't try to find out what happened?"

"Why should I?"

"I thought you were supposed to be protecting her?"

"She said she wanted protection, then she acted like she didn't need a damn thing. Look, I was worried about you, that's why I broke the speed limit in every town along the coast getting up here."

She slammed her hands on her hips. "And here you are now, sitting calmly having a beer with me when you know Lydia was afraid to talk to you because somebody was with her. What if it was the killer, you dumb shit?" Incredulity dripped from her words.

"Why shouldn't I be here with you?" I said. "I thought you were in trouble."

"Are you stupid? I'm not in trouble. If she knows who that

other Charlotte Randolph is, she could be the one in trouble. We'd better get down there and see if she's all right."

I picked up the phone and toggled up the long-distance operator, who put me through to Lydia's building. The man at the desk called her room but he got no answer.

"Did she go out?" I said.

"She may have, but I don't think so."

"Did she have any guests tonight?"

"Yes, as a matter of fact. A Mrs. Lester Randolph came to visit, but she left about six o'clock."

Oh, shit, I thought. That was about the time I called her. "Thanks," I said, and I hung up.

"Who was her guest?" Kitty asked.

I didn't answer just then, but I suspected the phony Mrs. Randolph had struck again.

CHAPTER 17

Kitty looked out over the dark ocean as we drove along the Pacific Coast Highway back to L.A. We said little, but as we approached West Hollywood, she asked if she could stay at my place.

"You might be safer at home," I said.

"During the day, maybe, but I'd feel safer with you at night." she said.

It was quite an admission after the fight we just had, but she was probably right. I might even be safer with the availability of two pairs of ears listening for strange noises, two pairs of eyes to see things out of order, and two of us to pick up on intuitive danger signals. On the last, Kitty would be better than me.

"Drop me off at my place, and I'll get my car," she said.

She already had my key, and I told her to let herself into my apartment. I was going to stop off to see Lydia first.

"So much for my nighttime safety," she said. It sounded like sarcasm, but the grin told me she was kidding.

It made no sense for me to check at the desk of Lydia's apartment hotel. It was well after midnight and they wouldn't let a man in her room that late. I sneaked along the pool in the rear of the building and counted off the rooms. The piece of tape was still stuck to window pane of her French doors.

There was no light from inside, so I jimmied the lock, found a lamp, and flicked it on. A quick look through the apartment showed me she wasn't there, but the place was as neat as if the maid had just finished cleaning. The dishes were put away and the ash trays were either emptied and cleaned or unused lately. There was a note pad beside the phone but there was nothing on it. Still, I slipped the pad into my jacket pocket. I checked the cabinets and drawers in her bedroom. Nothing seemed out of the ordinary, but that in itself was suspicious.

In the night table, I found the same kind of red-bordered manila envelope that held the photos of Kitty and Charlotte the Imposter. There were no photos in this envelope but there was a note on lavender paper: "Wouldn't it be nice for you if Toby Wentworth got a hold of these?"

I'd made an assumption that the notes to me and Lester Randolph were written by a man. This one was in the same handwriting, but I had different thoughts now. From the angle and awkwardness of the script, it looked like a normally right-handed person had tried to write left-handed.

As I slipped the note back into the envelope, I heard a click at the front door. I quickly slipped the envelope back into the drawer and hurried through the living room.

Two men were talking in the hallway as I moved quickly through the French doors and onto the patio. I stood back and watched as the big bald man from the front desk stepped into the apartment. Right behind him was Kansas and a uniformed cop. I watched from the edge of the pool, staying out of the glow of the interior light. They went into the bedroom and headed straight for a closet I hadn't gotten to yet.

Kansas looked down and shook his head, a sick look on his face. He turned away and reached for the phone, but before he touched it, he drew his hand back and said something to the uniformed cop, who left the room. I couldn't see into the closet, but I'd bet the fees on my next three jobs that he found the body of Lydia Lane.

I thought about my fingerprints in Lydia's apartment and about the fingerprints I expected the police to find on the gun that was stolen from my night table. The longer I waited, the more guilty I looked, so I decided that the appearance of stupidity was the better part of valor, and I stepped up to the French doors and tapped on the glass.

Kansas drew his revolver and swung back the door.

"What the hell you doing here?" he said.

"I'm surrendering," I said.

"What're you talking about?"

"It's a long story."

"Tell me about it later. I got a murder here."

"Lydia Lane?"

"I don't know for sure. You tell me."

He led me to the closet, and I looked down at the blonde who lay naked on a pile of shoes.

"That's her," I said. I had failed to protect her, but she hadn't given me much incentive. She didn't even seem to care.

"What the hell are you doing here?"

"I planned to talk to her, but I guess I'm a little late," I said, and I turned toward the door.

"Wait a minute." he said, grabbing my arm. "I want a better explanation than that."

Without mentioning either the real or the fake Charlotte Randolph, I explained as briefly as possible that Lydia had some information for me on the Noni Light murder. He chewed me out and said it was none of my business, and if I didn't stay out of his murder case, I might find myself arrested for obstruction, if not for the murders themselves.

I wanted to tell Kansas that my finger prints were all over

the apartment, and he would probably eventually find a snub-nose .38 that killed Noni Light with my prints and the smudge of somebody's gloves. I wanted to tell him that, but I didn't. It would just confuse the hell out of him and just might get me socked away for the rest of the night and most of tomorrow. I couldn't afford that, not with Kitty alone in my apartment.

"I'll stop by your office in the morning," I said.

"No," he said. "*I'll* stop by your office, and *you'd* better be there."

"Scouts honor," I said, throwing up three fingers on my right hand.

"Now get the hell out of here before I have to explain you to somebody," he said.

"Yes, sir."

"And stop being a smart ass."

"Right," I said, and I hurried out though the French doors, wondering why Kansas had let me off so easy.

When I got back to my apartment, Kitty jumped up from the sofa, her eyes bleary from sleep – or maybe from lack of it. She pointed the .45 Colt automatic I usually keep in the rack behind my bed.

"You claim you want to protect me and you're gone all God-damned night," she said. With the gun still in her hand, she crossed the room and put her arms around me.

"I wasn't gone all night. I was gone for an hour and a half," I said, and I peeled the .45 from her fingers.

"Was she there?"

"She's dead."

"You bastard," she said. She tried to slap me, but I grabbed her hand.

"I didn't do it for-crap-sake!"

"I sent her to you to protect her and you blew it," she said. There were tears in her eyes. "If you hadn't come running up the coast just because I didn't answer the phone, she might still be alive."

"I doubt it," I said. "Whoever killed her probably did it right after I called called. I couldn't have got there in time."

"You don't know that."

"No, I don't," I said, "but I've got a pretty good idea."

She opened her mouth to challenge, but she just let out a sigh. "Poor Lydia."

"Yeah. Poor everybody," I said. I put my arms around her and held her against my chest. "I found one of those envelopes like the one your pictures came in. Only this one didn't have any pictures. Just a note. I think it was the same handwriting."

"Somebody's blackmailing everybody."

"Yeah."

"That could've been me. Any one of them could've been me."

I knew what they all had in common, but I said nothing. I just held her for a long time while she sobbed into my jacket.

"I'm scared, Kane. I'm really scared."

I patted her for a long time. Then, finally, I scooped her off her feet and carried her to my bed. I laid her there and sat on the edge, smiling sadly.

"I'm scared too," I said. I was scared for all the women like Lydia and Jenny and Noni. The women who hung out with the stars and tried to catch their glitter. I felt sorry for the ones like Kitty who worked as call girls because they couldn't control their urge to be loved. I even felt sorry for those who did it just for the money. And Kitty fell into both categories. For 99% of them, nothing would ever work out. I hoped Kitty was among the 1% who was the exception.

She wouldn't look at me as I helped her out of her clothes

and covered her with the sheet. I undressed myself, turned off the lights, and slipped beside her in the bed. Holding her hands, I gently kissed her wet cheeks.

"I don't want to make love," she said.

"I know," I said.

There was a long period of silence. Finally, she began to speak the unspeakable conversation. "I love . . ."

She must have thought about it a long time, but when the time came, she still couldn't finish the sentence, and I was glad. If the words came out when we were making love, we could blame it on the passion of the moment. If our feelings ever came out in serious conversation, it might jinx everything there was between us. It was better left unsaid.

"We'll talk about it sometime," I said.

"No we won't. We'll never talk about that. We can't."

"I know."

The thing that the three starlets had in common with Kitty was the fact that they went to the same parties. Kitty was a call girl. The others were amateurs of sorts, and the odds were good they had made love to the same men from time to time. That was the similarity that bound them together. I fell asleep thinking about it.

I was up at seven, but Kitty was up before me getting ready for a modeling job. We were like a husband and wife, going about our business of getting ready for work as if the other didn't exist. She was the first to start through the door.

"Let's have lunch someplace," I said.

"I'll be working out of Finley's on Hollywood," she said.

"I'll meet you at Cristo's at noon," I said, and I pecked her lightly on the lips, a husbandly kiss if there ever was one.

That was the total of our morning conversation, but it scared me – especially the casual familiarity of the kiss.

The Big Switch

I sat in my office writing the names of people and places, writing dates and times, and in general trying to pull together all the information I had so I could go about finding what the hell was going on. Some of my thoughts were uncomfortable, some were downright weird, others made no sense at all. Murder never made sense.

At about nine-thirty, Kansas knocked at the door of my office, and I yelled for him to come in.

"Why the hell are you always sitting in your secretary's desk?" he asked as he stepped inside. He was chewing on a stub of his cigar.

"If I don't sit here, you sit here," I said. "Besides, I don't have a secretary."

"I know that, but at least you could give the right impression," he said as he slumped down into the soft, client chair I had moved from the back room. "It might be good for business."

"I've got all the business I can use," I said.

"You got all the work you can use. You got no business, and you got no business snooping around a dead broad's apartment. What were you doin' there?"

I told him most of it last night, and I repeated it, but I never got around to the confession part. I wasn't comfortable with it. I didn't always level with Kansas when our paths crossed, but I didn't usually let myself hang out on a plank the way I did this time. I sighed and looked him straight in the eyes.

"My finger prints are all over the place in there," I said. "I was looking around when you got there. I was only there a couple of minutes. I didn't find anything. I didn't even find the body."

"You told me that last night, but she died a long time before that. You told me twice you was working for her," he grumbled. "What were you supposed to be doing?"

It took me a couple of seconds to say the words. "I was supposed to be protecting her."

Kansas raised his brow.

"I didn't do such a good job," I said.

"No shit," he said.

"Thanks," I said. I didn't need to hear that from my friends. It was bad enough I kept telling myself that. He took the cigar out of his mouth and studied the soggy end. Finally, he shrugged, leaned forward and dropped it in the ashtray. Before he said another word, he took out a new cigar, peeled off the cellophane, and put the ring around the first digit of his little finger. Then he clamped the cigar between his teeth and held it there. It was his ritual of thought. Finally he took the cigar from his teeth and stared at the unlit end.

"How'd you know about the murder?" I said.

"Anonymous call."

"Man or woman?"

"Couldn't tell," he said. "So what else did you have on your mind last night?"

I was still afraid to tell him about the gun that the fake Mrs. Randolph planted on me, but if I waited any longer and it was found, I'd be suspect number one.

"I took possession of a snub-nose .38 after Noni was killed," I said, "but somebody stole it from me. I think it's the one being used for the killings. It's probably got my prints on it."

Kansas waited for a long time on that one. He even lit his cigar while he studied me.

"Was it licensed?"

"Not by me. I told you I took it from somebody."

"Who?"

"A client was waving it at me."

"Who?"

I should have carried this confession out to it's logical conclusion. Once I admitted to the gun and the prints, I had to explain a lot of cover ups or cover up some more, but I was already in too deep to add any new lies.

"I was working for a woman claiming to be Charlotte Randolph."

"'Claiming' to be Charlotte Randolph?"

"Yes," I said. "'Claiming.'"

Kansas' cheeks had already turned red, and he clamped down on the cigar so hard that he dripped saliva and tobacco from the corner of his mouth. He was measuring his response, trying to maintain his composure, his professionalism, and our friendship all at the same time. It was a tough rope to walk.

"So Noni Light gets killed, with a gun you think you handled and you don't tell me?"

"At that time, I didn't have the gun. I didn't have it until after the murder. I didn't even know she was dead when this woman planted it on me."

"'Planted' it on you?"

"She let me take it away from her," I said. I explained how I thought it was a plan and how it was stolen afterwards. I also explained that my prints should be pretty faded by now. "They might even be gone," I said.

"Kane, of all the weird things you've done, this might be the weirdest. Are you telling me we gotta look for a woman who *claims* to be Lester Randolph's wife?"

"Looks a *hell* of a lot like her."

Kansas took the cigar from his mouth again. This time, the ash was hot. "The guy on the desk at Lydia Lane's place says a woman claiming to be Mrs. Randolph visited her last night,"

Kansas said, seeking verification.

"I know."

"But you're telling me it's just somebody who looks like her."

"That's what I'm telling you," I said.

"I talked to Mrs. Randolph late last night," Kansas said. "She said she was in the middle of a kid's birthday party at six o'clock. Claims she didn't even know Lydia Lane."

I didn't reply.

"This woman who 'let' you take her gun. How do you know she's not Mrs. Randolph."

What could I do? Tell him about the blackmail photos Lester Randolph showed me of the fake? Confess that I'd made love to the real Charlotte Randolph and go into detail about the differences in the nipples and the relative weight of the two women? It might come to that, if I ever had to testify in court, or if I had to seriously defend myself, but it wasn't going to come to that if I could help it.

"I've met then both. They talk just slightly different. The imposter's got better diction."

"Than Mrs. Randolph?"

"Yes," I said.

He shrugged. "You got anything better than that?"

I remembered Noni Light's funeral, when the imposter planted herself next to Kansas in the back of the Chapel of Psalms. I told him about it, and he remembered me running from the chapel.

"Why didn't you tell me about this look-alike before?"

"I was working the case myself."

If he wasn't happy with me before, he was furious now. His face went so red, I thought he might have a stroke.

"Working on the case *yourself*?" he said. It was not just a question but an exclamation, perhaps an acknowledgement to himself that he heard what I said. He took a deep breath.

"'Working on the case yourself?' " he said. This time, it was a question.

"Yes."

"You son of a bitch," he said. Then he paused and said it again, even lower, more pronounced. "You stupid son of a bitch."

He stuffed the cigar between his molars. Then he rose and leaned forward, planting all ten of his fingers on the edge of my desk and glaring at me.

"Working on the case yourself?" he repeated still another time.

"Look, Kansas –"

"I'll look. You bet your ass, I'll look. I could get you for obstructing justice. Not just a little bit of obstruction, but a whole lot. Three murders we've got. Three! I could lock you up and throw the fucking key away!" he said. He didn't use that word very often and then only for extreme emphasis.

"I'm sorry."

"You're sorry," he said. Then he stood erect, lifted his hands from the desk and raised them to the heavens. "He's sorry," he said to Whoever was up there.

Trying very hard to retain his composure, he turned away and started for the door. Then he stopped and turned to me again in the slowly-I-turn tradition of a burlesque routine.

"Has it ever occurred to you," he said, "that if you had told me in the beginning, we might have saved the lives of these last two girls?"

I looked down at a cluster of dollar signs I had once inked on my desk blotter. He might be right. I doubted it, but he still made me feel like shit.

"What do you want me to say?" I asked.

"I don't want you to say anything. I want you to stop playing Sam Spade and work with me. We're friends, you and me. We've been through a lot together. You never did this to me before."

I did, but he didn't know about it. I'd pulled his ass out of the mud more than once, but he had me on this one. I was running around like a cowboy trying to find the crook because he didn't trust the local sheriff, and Kansas was one hell of a good sheriff, so to speak.

"I'm sorry," I said again.

That was my sole defense. The worst part about it was that there was more I could tell him, maybe more I *should* tell him, but we were getting down to the wire now, and I didn't want the cops to blow the case for me.

"You're sorry?" he said. He turned away, shaking his head and left my office without closing the door.

"Sorry?" I heard him mutter again in disgust as he started down the stairs to Sunset Boulevard. "All he says is he's sorry."

CHAPTER 18

I was still struggling with the facts when the phone rang, and I was greeted with the soft, yet throaty "Hello" of the real Charlotte Randolph.

"Hi," I said in my cheeriest voice, but she got right down to business.

"You got my pictures yet?" she said.

"Not yet," I said, trying to keep the smile in my voice. "I haven't had the right opportunity."

"I want 'em in the next couple of days, or I want my money back," she said. Her voice was still soft and there was no urgency in her tone, but the demand was clear. The problem was that I'd already spent a lot of her money just to make ends meet and I didn't want to go into the savings Kitty had worked so hard to get me started on.

"I'll see what I can do," I said. "When can I see you?"

"For what purpose?"

"Well, uh . . ." I thought of Kitty, felt guilty, and let my words trail off.

"I'll see you 'that way' again when you have the pictures," she said.

Beautiful or not, wonderful mother and housewife or not, great lay or not, right now, she was a bitch who meant business.

"I'll get them," I said, and I hung up. "I got to get into another line of work," I muttered to myself.

It was stupid. I should've gotten pictures of Lester with Lydia when I had the chance, but I had been too wrapped up in trying to find who killed Noni Light.

I grabbed my jacket and started for the door. On my way down the stairs, I realized something was swinging in my coat pocket, and I found the note pad I'd picked up near Lydia's telephone. I was so panicked last night when Kansas came into her room that I forgot about it and hadn't given it a thought since. I tossed it on the passenger side and climbed behind the wheel of my '48 Ford.

Kitty was not yet at Cristo's when I arrived, so I took Lydia's pad and gently rubbed over it with the graphite from the stub of my #2 lead pencil. The idea was to bring out the impression of whatever had been written on the page preceding it. It usually didn't turn up anything, but this time it worked, but all I came up with was a list:

> *Meeting with Mr. Wrenking*
> *Touch up roots*
> *Curls?*
> *Blue skirt? Red skirt?*
> *White blouse.*
> *Nice shoes.*

A list, only a list, but it left me with questions of why Dick Wrenking wanted to see her? It might have something to do with the Calamity Jane picture, I thought as I tore off the top sheet, folded it, and put it in my shirt pocket. I slipped the pad back into my jacket pocket and ordered a Johnny Walker Red and soda.

"Waiting long?" said Kitty, seating herself across the booth from me.

She looked terrific in her yellow dress and small lace hat, and I told her her that, but the outfit looked more like something for a Sunday afternoon. I didn't tell her that, but she must have picked up something in my attitude, and she felt a need to explain.

"It's one of the outfits I'm modeling," she said. "I didn't have time to change."

Apparently I hurt her feelings. "You want a drink?"

"Not when I'm working. Not modeling anyhow."

"What did Kansas have to say?" she asked, after we ordered a glass of iced tea and a Monte Cristo sandwich for her, and an iced tea and a rare roast beef for me.

I laughed ironically and told her about my meeting with him this morning. "He told me to be a good boy and not to hide things from him anymore."

"And?"

"I promised," I said.

"He doesn't believe it any more than you do," she said, with a chuckle. Then she sighed. "Did he say anything new about who killed Lydia?"

I reached into my pocket and pulled out the note page over which I had brushed the graphite. I unfolded it and explained how I got it. I told her what it said and what I thought it might mean.

"Did you tell Kansas?"

"I forgot all about it until a little while ago."

"He'll love you for that."

"Maybe I'd better take it over to him."

"He'll love that too." She was right. Kansas hated afterthoughts.

"Maybe I won't then. Look, we've got three murders here, but I only know two of the three women. What did you know about Jenny James?"

"Toby Wentworth," she said.

"What?"

The waiter brought our iced tea and sandwiches. Kitty looked at the food and tasted the tall iced tea through a straw, while I reached for the sugar.

"She was at Toby's party," she said.

"I thought you said –"

"I know what I said, and I also know what I know. Jenny was there, but when she was there, she was a brunette like you said."

"Why didn't you tell me that?"

"I'm not sure," she said. Finally, she looked directly into my eyes and explained. "I'm not even sure I knew when you asked me."

"What do you know now?"

"She left the party with Roger Francene."

"Roger?"

"Yes. Homosexual Roger."

"Where did they go? What did they do?"

"I didn't follow them, for God sakes!"

I didn't want to press her, but I couldn't help myself. "Kitty, you're not stupid. Why didn't you tell me?"

"Don't you listen? I didn't even know it. It just started to come back to me this morning when one of the girls I work with came in with a different color hair."

"Does Roger sail or anything?"

"Only in the movies."

"But not on a boat?"

"I don't think so, but I don't know Roger that well. I'm not his type. Not young enough or small enough."

But the other three were, I thought. Somebody got Jenny James on a boat and got her bitten by a shark between the party and the time she was washed up on the beach. Somebody also went to the trouble of making her look like Kitty – a lot like

Kitty. Now, I wanted to get to the bottom of it before she got hurt.

After we ate, Kitty said she'd meet me at my apartment tonight, and we said good bye. Then I went over to Morgan Studios. I hoped to use Lester Randolph as an entree to the studio, but he wasn't in, and I was unable to get onto the lot.

A few phone calls told me that Lydia Lane's list that included Dick Wrenking might have been a fantasy note to herself – or maybe somebody was pulling a deadly trick on her. No one in Wrenking's office had ever heard of her.

"How about in your starlet pool?"

"That's not Mr. Wrenking's department," the secretary intoned sweetly.

"If you come up with something, please let me know."

"We certainly will, Mr. Kane."

I left both my apartment and office numbers with her, but I didn't expect to hear anything. Hollywood, like every place else in show business, was full of the "Don't call us, we'll call you" mentality.

"Is Mr. Francene on the lot?" I asked the Morgan gate guard.

"He's only here when he's doing a picture."

Roger Francene knew I wasn't a cop, but I decided to give it another shot. When I knocked on his front door, the handsome young butler told me he was not to be disturbed. I said it was important, but that didn't impress him.

"Just announce me," I said.

"He knows you're here," the boy snarled.

I pushed forward and he tried to stop me. He had plenty of brawn and lots of mouth, but not much will. It was like pushing and old lady.

"Where is he?" I said, once I was in the entry hall.

"He's not here."

"Than how does he know I'm here."

"He . . . I . . ." He was nearly in tears, and I almost felt sorry for him.

"I'll have to get you a gun," Roger said from the timbered balcony over the entry hall. He was wrapped in a gray silk robe.

"I've got some more questions."

"I don't have to answer your questions," he said.

"I understand you left Toby's party Sunday night with Jenny James."

"You understand wrong," he said.

"The police don't know that yet," I said. "Would you like to talk to me about it first?"

There was a pause, then Roger spoke: "Get Mr. Kane a drink. Scotch is it?"

"With ice," I said.

"I'll just have a glass of water," Roger said.

The butler looked at me, then at Roger. Reluctantly, he went to the back of the house.

"He is a nice boy. Honestly," Roger said, as he descended the stairs with the majesty of a queen. He led me to the chairs in front of the huge living room fireplace.

"Now where did you hear this damnable lie?"

"A little bird told me."

"Well, tell your little bird she's mistaken."

"How did you know it was a she-bird."

"All birds are she's," he said. He was showing yet another personality. It wasn't that he thought he was different people, it was just that he took on a different aspect each time I talked to him.

"Was Jenny James a blonde or a brunette when you saw her last?"

He laughed through his nose and crossed his legs, letting one of his knees peek from under the robe. Demurely he covered it and sighed. "For some reason, she was a brunette. How did you know?"

"Where did you take her?"

"Here, of course."

"And?"

"You don't really don't know me, do you Mr. Kane?"

I didn't reply. I knew he went both ways but I also knew his preference was men.

"How did butler-boy feel about that?"

"What butler-boy doesn't know, doesn't hurt him," he said, finishing up just a few seconds before the young man came back with my Scotch and Roger's water. No one spoke as he handed us the drinks. Then Roger dismissed him. The boy wanted to speak, but he knew it would be out of place, and he glided from the room with Roger watching every move of his behind. He was Roger's current adventure.

"When was the last time you saw Jenny James?"

"Nine a.m., Monday. I put her in a cab."

"Just like Noni," I said, and I took a swallow of my drink.

"What is that supposed to mean?"

"Was Toby here?" I said, ignoring his question.

He sighed and waited. "Of course not."

"Was anyone else here?"

"Bennie, the butler."

"Do you know where the cab took her?"

"Home, I suppose."

"Which was where?"

"Venice," he said.

That could explain a lot and it could explain nothing. In any event, I wondered why Kansas hadn't offered me that piece of information. I also wondered why she didn't live in the same hotel with Noni and Lydia.

"Did she swim?"

"Certainly. Max loaned her out for several of Esther Williams' films."

"Does she boat or sail?"

"If someone took her," he said. Clearly, he was implying Lester Randolph. "You know, Mr. Kane, you're asking an awful lot of questions that would be better asked by the police. I'm sure they have someone who will come to see me. But you do suspect me, don't you?"

"I do."

"How exciting," he said, leaning toward me and fluttering his eye lashes. He was now playing the role of the queen on the make, but he was less interested in me than in young starlets he teased. It was his way of showing anger.

"Aren't you afraid to be revealed to the rest of the world?" I said.

"I've lived like this since before the war. Have you ever read anything about how . . . I am?"

"Nope."

"You see it's just rumor. Only rumor. And you've heard that same rumor about every other good-looking male star in Hollywood. This new fellow – Rock Hudson, is it? They've started it about him some, but the rumors will die out and every one will forget about it. Who would believe you if you told the public that I was homosexual, Mr. Kane? It would just be chalked up as another rumor."

"I wasn't threatening. When's the last time you spoke to your sister?"

"Please finish your drink," he said.

Roger gave me nothing more of value, but as drove to the West Hollywood address of my nickel crooks, I wondered if he had learned something from me.

CHAPTER 19

Clarita Drive was not far from Beverly Hills in distance, but a world away in style. The house sat high on an incline, and was little more of a cottage with an attic. There was no limo on the sloping driveway, a sign that nobody was home, so it was a good time to look.

I parked my Ford in the next block, and like a bill collector I walked up to the front door and knocked several times. When I got no answer, I jimmied the easy lock without taking off my suede gloves and slipped the pick set into my pocket.

I stepped into the cluttered living room. "Anybody home?" I called, just like I belonged there.

As expected, there was no answer.

The furniture was shabby but not at all cheap. It looked like the owners had bought it at one of the estate sales where Kitty selected my furniture. I moved quickly through all the rooms to make certain no one was home, and I planned my escape in case someone came back before I was finished with what I had to do.

There was no doubt it was a man's house. There were dirty ashtrays, dishes in the sink and dust on just about everything. I rummaged through the downstairs room, looking through drawers, under furniture, even under rugs. I looked in the only vase and in the two covered pots under the sink. I found nothing downstairs but I hit the mother lode when I started through the first of the two upstairs bedrooms. One of them was peculiarly feminine. It was something I didn't notice on the first rush through the house. In the closet, I found both women's and men's clothes, as if the room were shared by two people. A quick look at the men's things told me they probably belonged to Cheeves, the one who was the chauffeur and the male model in the Charlotte imposter's blackmail photos.

They weren't wide enough for Wells. The woman's things consisted of sweaters, skirts, shoes and hats – including the outfit the imposter had worn to Noni Light's funeral. There was also a pair of gloves that looked like the ones the imposter wore while holding the snub-nose .38 on me. I was tempted to take them, but I didn't.

My first assumption was that the Charlotte Randolph imposter shared Cheeves' room, but when I looked through the bureau and chest of drawers, I noticed a peculiar lack of men's underwear. That could have a lot of meanings, only a few of which made sense. I filed the information in my memory for future use, went over to the roll-top desk, and used my small skeleton key, which opened just about any desk in town.

Inside the desk were a mirror and enough grease paint and rouge to make up the entire chorus of a Toby Wentworth musical. In the top middle drawer, I found a stack of black and white, eight by ten glossies of naked women: some of women with Cheeves, some with women alone.

The glossies included Noni, Lydia, Kitty, Gloria Hastings and Jenny James as a blonde, but there were a lot of other women too. There were also a set of the same photos Lester Randolph had shown me of his wife's imposter. There were a lot of photos. I took one of each woman, rolled them and creased them. Then I stuffed them into my inside breast pocket.

In one of the side drawers was as a half-full box of .38

caliber shells. As I slipped one of them into my jacket, I heard a car coming up the driveway. Quickly, I tried to put everything the way I found it. Then going down the stairs hip-first, I skipped two steps at a time, and in four strides I was in the living room. I started for the back of the house, but I heard Wells and Cheeves' voices as they walked around the side toward the back way. I reversed myself and exited by the front door. Then I trotted up the street in the gathering dusk. It would not take them long to realize someone had been in the house.

I drove to the next street before I started looking for a phone booth. I called my apartment but Kitty wasn't there yet, so I called Charlotte.

"Is your husband home?" I said,

"The children are," she said firmly, as if she were telling me to get lost.

"That's not why I'm asking," I said, making it clear I wasn't coming over to see her. "I'm trying to get those pictures you wanted."

"Try the boat," she said, bitterly.

The boat again. The god dammed boat. What was it about the boat? I was about to earn Charlotte's money, most of which I had already spent.

It was after dark when I found Gloria Hastings' pre-war Continental parked on the lot behind the marina. I had little doubt who she was visiting. I slung my Leica with flash over my shoulder and paced onto the pier as if I owned not just a boat but the whole damn place. I didn't change my pace but I walked softer as I approached Lester's boat. Then I slowed to a stop, pretending to admire the red moon rising over the swamp that somebody was trying to turn into a boater's paradise. As soon as I saw the gentle rocking of the boat, I stepped on the deck.

"What was that?" Lester said, and he moved quickly and rocked the boat further. They were in the master suite. If Lester chose to investigate, he had me, but I sat still, waiting. He never showed up and after a while, they went back to the gentle rock, rocking of the hull, which could be caused by only a few things, and I had a pretty good idea which of those it was.

I walked at pace with the rocking as I crossed the afterdeck and stepped into the salon. I unshouldered the Leica and the rocking stopped.

So did I.

"Let me go see if anybody's out there," Lester said.

"There's nobody out there. You're a ninny," Gloria Hastings growled. "Ever since that Jenny James thing, you've been scared to death."

"How would you like to be suspected of three murders?"

"Nobody suspects you," she said.

"Not until the last one. Let me just take a look."

"Shut up and get back here."

"But –"

There was a sudden jolt, as if she pulled him to her. That was exactly like the Gloria Hastings who I made love to a few days ago. I waited again, and after some non-synchronous rocking, they were back to the gentle rock-rock of what they were doing before Lester panicked. The tempo increased to a more rapid rock, more rapid breathing.

"Let's . . . go out . . . on the water," Gloria said, and I waited.

"Not now . . . not now," he said. "Not . . . oh, God!"

It was time for pictures.

I kicked open the door and snapped the first photo with

Lester looking at me over his shoulder. I wasn't sure I got Gloria at all, and I quickly replaced a flash bulb, but by the time I did, Lester was up, naked and reaching for me. Gloria was in the viewfinder, making no effort to cover herself.

"Who the hell are you?" she shouted, as I snapped the second photo. The lights blinded them and neither one would recognize me. I went with a well-placed kick in Lester's abdomen and sent him sprawling sideways over Gloria as I loaded the third bulb.

The third photo was a dilly.

I hurried out of the cabin, up the companionway, through the salon, across the deck, and onto the pier.

"Wait! I'll pay you," Lester called, as I trotted toward the front gate. There was a better than excellent chance they wouldn't come naked across the planks just to see who I was.

"Hey you?" the custodian called from his little hut at the gate, but I was already cutting through the undergrowth to the place where I had parked my Ford on the road into Venice.

I took the film to a newspaper friend of mine, but only to get them developed and printed. Then I hurried home to Kitty. She peeked out to make sure it was me before she unhooked the burglar chain.

"Somebody keeps calling and hanging up," she said.

It was me they were after. "Maybe you'd be safer at home," I said.

"I'm not afraid of some damned obscene caller."

"It might be more than that."

"You've been a detective too long."

Yeah, I thought, but how else could I make a decent living with prices shooting up the way they were?

I slipped the eight by ten glossies out of the envelope and tossed them out on the kitchen table.

"Nice action shots," Kitty said.

"Look at these," I said and I pulled the ones I got from Wells and Cheeves' place from another envelope. They were rolled and curled and creased in segments from having been in my pocket, so they didn't lay flat. I got the envelope from my friend down at the paper.

"I'll take two of this one," Kitty said, picking up the one of herself. It had obviously been taken at the same time as the others they had tried to blackmail me with.

I pointed to the one of Jenny James. "Is that her?"

"Yes."

I looked at the photo and looked at Kitty. The only things missing were the high cheekbones of a model. Their noses were similar, straight and smallish. Kitty's lips were slightly fuller but the make-up artist who did Jenny for death had taken care of that.

"She does look like me."

"They fooled the hell out of me for a couple of seconds," I said.

I showed Kitty the .38 caliber shell and told her where I got it.

"I think you should take it all down to Kansas and tell him everything. Finish it up, now!"

"Why?"

"Because somebody means business, and their business is to frame you for everything."

The phone rang and she looked at me.

"Pick it up and treat them the way you've been treating them all night," I said.

She smiled, picked up the phone and let out a string of profanity that would have done a top sergeant proud.

"Oh," she said at the end. Her cheeks tinged peach and she held the phone in my direction. "It's for you."

I held back a laugh but she slammed me on the biceps with the side of her fist. On the other end of the line was Charlotte Randolph.

"Is that your mother?" Charlotte said, sarcastically.

"The maid," I said, and Kitty slammed me again. I smirked and pushed her hand away. "What can I do for you?"

"Lester just came home, and he's upset."

"He should be."

"Did you get 'em?"

"I got them," I said.

"Good," she said. "The kids leave for school at eight-thirty in the morning. They ain't back till three. Bring the pictures."

The way she said it almost required a "Yes, ma'am," but I avoided the temptation. "Yeah."

I hung up and Kitty smirked.

"Anybody I know?" she said.

"Mrs. Randolph."

"The one in the pictures?"

"No, the real one."

CHAPTER 20

"That'll show you, you bastard," Lester Randolph said from the afterdeck of his boat. I was treading water, naked except for a necklace of chicken guts. Other chicken parts floated in the water and three sharks swam around in me in ever tightening circles.

"You've got no one to blame but yourself," the fake Charlotte Randolph called from the foredeck. She smiled, ready to use the snub-nose .38 that dangled from her fingers.

"Brian!" I heard Kitty call, but I couldn't see her. If I swam for it, the sharks would certainly get me, and if they didn't, the Charlotte Randolph imposter would. But if I stayed still, I had no chance at all. I ripped the chicken-gut necklace away from me, tossed it into the distance, and swam for the boat. One of the sharks grabbed me by the shoulder and started to shake me.

"Brian!" Kitty shouted.

The shark was dragging me under.

"Brian," Kitty insisted, shaking me by the shoulder.

I sat upright in bed.

"Wake up. Somebody's trying to get in," she said.

"Thank God!" I said, still not feeling totally safe from the sharks.

"You've been dreaming. Somebody's trying to get in!"

My entire body was soaked with perspiration, and I let out

a long sigh as I sat up. Dream or not, I was glad to be out of that water.

"What?" The dream was gone, but it took a moment for me to understand what she was talking about.

"Somebody's trying to break in," she said.

Finally I understood. I was out of the dream and into reality. I listened for a few seconds, but I heard nothing but the ticking of the clock on the night table. Just to be safe, I reached back to the rack behind the headboard and grabbed the Colt Automatic.

"Stay here," I whispered.

I moved softly through the bedroom. I stopped at the door and listened but I heard nothing. I moved against the wall, stopped again, listened again. Still, I heard nothing. Through the darkness, I eased through every room in the apartment but I found nobody, nothing. I flicked on the lights and again moved through the rooms. The photos were still on the desk in the living room. The .38 shell was still in the night table. The only thing out of order was the burglar chain, which was unhooked and dangling against the doorframe. They must have come in through the window, gone out through the door. Or the whole thing might just be Kitty's imagination, I thought, but I was still uncomfortable.

"I know I heard something," Kitty said, when I told her everything was all right.

"Yeah," I said, as if I thought she were crazy. It was better to let her believe that than to let her stay afraid. I looked at the clock: twenty after five. I tried to get back to sleep but it was impossible. Light was starting to creep though the shade. I lay still for a while, then I got out of bed and went into the kitchen. I wanted to put down all the facts so I could sort out the important from the trivial, but I had nothing to write on. I went to the bedroom closet and took Lydia Lane's note pad from the pocket of my jacket.

"Can't sleep?" Kitty asked.

"Time to get up anyway."

She flicked on the light and looked at the clock. "You're right. I got to get to work."

Naked, she padded across the floor to the bathroom and started the shower.

"Want to join me?" she said.

Under normal circumstances she wouldn't have to ask the first time.

"I got too much on my mind," I said, and I carried the pad into the kitchen. I listed the names of everybody I suspected and some I didn't. I listed potential motives. I even considered that different people committed the murders.

Lester Randolph came up an important suspect. So did the real Charlotte. Roger Francene and Toby Wentworth were high on my list, and Wells and Cheeves could be working for any of them. I even listed Kansas as a suspect along with some others I had stumbled across here and there. I used the first two sheets on the pad, and when I peeled to the third sheet. I raised my eyebrows in surprise.

"What's the matter?" said Kitty, who had just come into the kitchen. She had her robe drawn tightly around her, and for the first time, I realized she had picked up a few pounds since I first met her.

"You look even worse now. What is it?" she said.

"Take a look," I said, sliding the pad across the porcelain surface of the table.

"What does it mean?" she said.

"I think it's Lydia's handwriting," I said. A name was scribbled quickly across the page.

"Who's Carla Mahoney?" said Kitty.

"I don't know. She might not be important at all, but if

Lydia scribbled it down when I was talking to her on the phone, it could be the name of the fake Charlotte Randolph."

"It could be Lydia's real name too."

"Could be a lot of things. Look, can I borrow your car today? I'll take you to work."

"Go to hell," she said.

I explained that if I had to go into Beverly Hills on the sly, my Ford would attract too much attention. "The Beverly Hills cops might be onto it already, and you know how nasty they get."

"Why don't you get yourself a nicer car," she grumbled, but she came back from the bedroom and tossed me her keys. "You be careful."

"Get dressed. We'll have breakfast someplace."

While Kitty got herself prettied up for her daytime job, I went over my list and I looked at the photos. Some had been retouched, and there were other things in them I hadn't thought much about before, and I wondered if somebody was paying extortion.

I was met by a smiling Charlotte Randolph, who was wearing that silver-gray robe that was her uniform. I had the feeling she had dozens of them. I handed her the envelope with the three eight-by-then photos of Lester and Gloria Hastings.

Still standing in the entry hall, she shuffled through them several times, and each time she went to the next picture, the expression on her lips curled more viciously.

"That bastard," she said, and she looked up, fire in her eyes.

Right now, she was terribly exciting, but I was not about to make any suggestions that would result in having my severed private parts presented to me in Charlotte's bloody hands.

"You can mail me a check for the rest," I said.

"What?" she said.

"I said, 'You can mail me a check for the rest.'"

From the way she glared at me, I thought she meant she didn't owe me any more money, and I would have a hell of a time collecting it.

But I was mistaken.

"Come on in," she said, and she walked straight up the stairs to her four-poster bed.

"How much will the balance be?" she said.

I told her.

"That much?"

"A man's got to make a living."

"'A man's got to make a living?'" she said and she started to laugh. "Would you do me a favor and write that down? I want to put it in my screenplay."

I thought she was kidding until we were in her bedroom and she reached in her night table and took out a pad and paper.

"Please," she said. "And sign it. I'll give you a little footnote."

Everybody out here was writing a screenplay, I thought as I wrote the phrase and signed it.

When I came up from the night table, she put her left hand behind my head and put her face to mine. Her kiss was soft and wet as her right hand slid over the back of my left thigh and to my buttocks, squeezing hard.

"This is going to be a day you'll never forget," she growled, and she was absolutely right. The sex was so vicious and so exciting, I almost wanted to go out and take another set of pictures.

❖

It was the middle of the afternoon before I got to Kansas' office, and he was not at all happy to see me.

"What do you want?" he said, not looking up from his paper work.

"I want to find out how you're making out on the Jenny James case.

"Fine," he said. He planted his elbows on his desk. He fingered his yellow pencil between his hands and tilted his head to the side in an expression of contrived sarcasm. "And how are *you* making out on the Noni Light case?"

"I was going to ask you about that too, and about Lydia Lane while we're at it."

"Why should I bother? You're a one-man show. What the hell do you need the Los Angeles Police Department for? Why doesn't the mayor just hire you to solve all our murders?"

"What's the matter? Did you forget to eat lunch?"

He let out a long puff of breath and slapped his pencil to his desk. "What the hell do you think's the matter? I'm running three murder investigations, and I got a free-lance jerk who thinks he's Philo Vance, Sam Spade and Casey Crime Photographer all wrapped up in one."

I wondered if he knew about the pictures.

"You're running around town pretending to be a cop, and I'm getting complaints from the mayor and the Beverly Hills Police Department. You got more information than I got, and I want it *all.*"

"I'm working on a case of my own," I said.

"Yeah? Who's paying you to find Noni Light's killer?"

"Privileged information." Now that I had delivered the photos of Gloria Hastings and Lester, I was off that case, but I wasn't about to give up until I had the killer.

"Bull shit. I want everything you got," he said. "Beverly Hills got a complaint that one of *their* men has been hassling a certain Hollywood musical director. But they think he's from my department. A guy named Kane, just Kane. But I checked and the only Kane or Cain or anything like that is working the streets down in Lakewood. Where the hell do you come from passing yourself off as a cop?"

"Kansas, we've been through this before. I knock on somebody's door and tell them I'm working on the Noni Light murder. People just naturally want to talk to me. Nobody asks me for a badge. If they do, I can't show them one, so I tell them I'm a private detective. Then they either cooperate, or they don't. When they don't, I walk away. Why don't we just work together like always?"

"And we been through this before too. I'd love to work with you, but you don't work *together*. You don't tell me shit. All we got is ballistics on a .38 caliber shell. You got information about parties and boat trips and God-knows-what-all."

I wondered where he had information about the boat trip, and if he had the same information I had. If he did, why didn't he put Lester Randolph and his boat together and come up with a suspect for the Jenny James killing? But maybe he did.

"What do you got to say for yourself?" he said, as if he were talking to a kid.

"What do you want me to say?"

"Just give me what you've got."

"I gave you a list of my suspects. What else do you want?"

"I'll give you everything after you tell me what you've got," he said.

"No deal," I said.

"You want me to get you for impersonating a police officer?"

"I didn't impersonate an officer. I just let them believe it," I countered. "What do you know? What's this stuff about boat trips?"

"You tell me," he said.

"*You* tell *me.*"

It was ping-pong.

"This is getting us no place," he said, and he started to wave his pencil at me. "If you impersonate a cop one more time, I'm going to throw your ass in jail."

He was pointing the pencil at me. If he wasn't a cop, I'd have taken it away from him and stuffed it up his nose, but like a good little boy, I waited until he was finished.

"Lester Randolph was out on his boat for two days," I said. "He came in about the same time Jenny James' body was found. What do you know about boats?"

"Randolph, huh?"

"Randolph," I said.

"What makes you think he had Jenny James with him?"

"I didn't say that. I just think the timing of his coming into port is interesting."

"Yeah. Damned interesting. How'd you get that?"

"I asked at the marina."

Kansas had mellowed out, and I didn't quite know why. Maybe I gave him something. I used patience and waited. After about thirty seconds, it worked.

"Did he spend a lot of time on his boat?" Kansas said after a long pause.

"Not last week. This week quite a bit," I said.

"Do I have your word that nothing I tell you goes out of this office?"

"You got my word," I said.

He gave me a lot of things I knew and some I didn't know. For one thing, he had somebody doing surveillance on Toby Wentworth's party. There were other starlets beside Jenny and Lydia. Gloria Hastings was there and so was Roger Francene and Lester Randolph.

"There was also a couple of junior crooks who just got fired from Warners, names of Wells and Cheeves."

"Who were they with?" I said.

"Limo service for Roger Francene."

I hoped the surprise didn't show on my face, but he picked it up. "Kitty was there too," I said, trying to give a different meaning to the look.

Kansas made a face. It was a fact he was trying to keep from me, probably because he didn't want me to be hurt.

"How do you know?" he said.

"She told me," I said. Actually, it was Lydia who told me. Kitty just verified it.

"How long did the party last?" I said.

"Till morning. They always last till morning."

"Where'd Kitty go afterwards?" I said.

"We don't know. All we know is she left early with Lydia Lane and Lester Randolph."

"They went to Randolph's boat," I said, so he wouldn't have to feel like a liar if he had held that back from me. "Were there any makeup people there? Any artists?"

"I don't know," he said. "I don't know what half of these flakes do. The only ones I know are the actors."

"Good idea to find out," I said. "Especially the way Jenny James was made up. When did Randolph's boat go out?"

"I don't know for sure. Could've been late Monday,"

"What do you know for sure?" I said.

"There was some guy on the boat in drag," he said.

"How did your man know it was a guy in drag?"

"No man can walk in heels, not even a fairy."

I thought about the women's clothes in Wells and Cheeves' house and about the makeup in the roll-top desk. It was the kind of thing I should give Kansas, but I didn't want him to know I been in there, so I had to hold it back a bit longer.

Kansas continued to talk, and I continued to hear the words, but none of it was new, and I was thinking about all the things to check yet. Kansas finished with a lecture and told me to make damn sure I gave him anything new I found. I stopped in the lobby of City Hall and looked up Carla Mahoney in the phone directory. The only one in the book showed the same address as Wells and Cheeves, and somehow, it didn't surprise me.

I picked Kitty up at the department store where she was working, and took her to dinner. I drank nothing but coffee and I told her some of what I thought. "I still need your car," I said.

"I still think you're crazy," she said, but she let me keep it a while longer.

That night, I made certain my .38 Special was fully loaded and racked in my shoulder holster when I dove alone into West Hollywood. As I approached Wells and Cheeves' place. The lights beamed out between the curtains of the house, and the limo was in the driveway, but it now had Illinois plates.

My plan was to park a hundred yards away and try to see what was going on inside, but as I drove past the house, I saw Billy Wells and Teddy Cheeves coming down the front steps.

And behind them was the Charlotte Randolph imposter.

I drove by slowly and looked in the rear-view mirror. A half block away, I turned off my lights and pulled to the curb. Cheeves opened the back door for them. Then he pulled out of the driveway and started in my direction. I slumped down in the seat and waited until they passed. Then I started after them. A few blocks later, I flicked on the lights and followed them into Beverly Hills. I was surprised when they stopped at the gate of Toby Wentworth's white mansion, where Carla Mahoney, or whoever it was, got out, stepped through the pedestrian gate and hurried up the walk. I pulled to the curb, turned out my lights, and watched in the rear view mirror.

After the limo pulled away, I walked back and climbed the fence. My guess was that she would head right for Toby Wentworth's bedroom. I calculated where that would be from the general placement of the rooms and from the light that showed outside. When I came here during the day, I saw no hint of an alarm system, and I had confidence I could get through undetected. I jimmied my way easily through the French doors at the top of the wide stairway over the pool.

I felt certain the woman I was following was the Carla Mahoney of Lydia's quickly scratched note, as well as the Charlotte Randolph impostor.

The back stairs were where I expected them to be, and I worked my way to the second floor. I eased along the upstairs hallway. In the all white house, it was hard to hide, even at night.

"Of course I can't give you a part, but not that kind of part," Toby said. "The studio heads would never stand for it and people wouldn't buy it."

I didn't hear the reply.

"I don't care how well you test. It won't make any difference. I'm sorry, I can't help you," he said, and I heard clack of a telephone being cradled.

"Who was that?" said whoever was with him.

"Just another one of those bitches," Toby said.

"But you've got so many of them," said the other.

There was a pause for the rustle of clothes. I waited, listening. Finally, I went to the keyhole, feeling more like a peeping Tom than a detective.

"You're so good at this," Toby Wentworth said gleefully, before I even got an angle on them.

Then I felt a crash at the back of my head.

Later, I had to reconstruct a lot of what happened, because a whole lot was fuzzy. The next thing I knew, I was slumped on the horn of Kitty's car with the top down, and Kansas was shaking me conscious. I was parked in front of my own apartment building.

"You're going downtown," he said.

"What for?"

"You're under arrest for the murders of Noni Light, Lydia Lane, and Jenny James," he said.

"What the hell are you talking about? How did I get here?" I said. I felt the back of my head. There was no blood, but there was a lot of swelling.

"You were sitting here," he said.

"Knocked out?" I said, but as the words slipped through my lips, I smelled the reek of stale Scotch.

"Wait a minute. I haven't had anything to drink."

"Sure," said Kansas, and he snapped a cuff around my wrist.

"This is crazy," I said.

"Yep," Kansas said. "I never thought you were the killer type."

"I'm not. You know me."

"Nobody knows anybody," he said. He dragged me at first. Then he just led me to my own apartment. Kitty was sitting in one of the living room chairs, gripping the arm rests. I could tell by the way she jumped up and rushed to me that she hadn't said a word to Kansas.

"They searched the place. They came in and searched the place," she said, putting her arms around me.

"They didn't find anything," I said.

"Come here," said Kansas, leading me into the kitchen.

On the table were the rolled-up photos I took from Wells' place. Next to it was a box of shells like the one I saw at Wells' place and a snub-nose .38.

"I don't even carry a snub-nose," I said.

"But you told me you handled one," said Kansas. "My bet is this is it."

"This is ridiculous."

Kansas took me to police headquarters, but he didn't question me – at least not at first. He turned me over to Derinzi, who worked under him in homicide. It wasn't the first time I was questioned by him, nor did I expect it to be the last. I didn't like Derinzi, and he didn't like me. He took me into an interrogation room and sat me on a chair under a naked light bulb.

"Where's the rubber hose?" I said.

"Comes later," said Derinzi, who was smoking like a Texas barbecue and making sure the smoke got in my face.

"How'd that stuff get into your apartment?"

"What stuff?" I said just to get an inventory of what they found or thought they found. He named nothing that surprised me, including the snub-nose .38.

"Well?" Derinzi said.

"Must've been planted," I said.

"Sure, sure. We're checking the gun now. Bet we find your prints all over it."

"I don't doubt it," I said.

"What's that supposed to mean?"

I shrugged. I didn't know if Kansas had already told him, so I went through the story of the Charlotte Randolph imposter and how she set me up.

"You expect me to believe that crap?" Derinzi said.

"Why not? I'm sure Kitty told you about somebody trying to break in last night."

"So?" he said, verifying it. He blew smoke in my face again. I knew the plan: he knew I was a smoker and I was supposed to crumble because I needed a cigarette. I smoke a lot, but I'm not about to confess to something I didn't do just because I want a cigarette. I have no idea what kind of idiot that works with, but I suppose it does sometimes.

"That's probably when they planted the gun," I said. I wasn't worried about the shells they found. I carried a .38 myself, and they fit just fine with my .38 Special. Wells, or whoever, planted them just to get them out of his own place.

"You got a good imagination," said Derinzi. "You know that?"

"No better than whoever set me up."

He chuckled. He loved every second of this, and it wasn't the first time he interrogated me. What he hated was that, so far, he had never been able to pin anything on me. I'd never even been indicted on anything, but he smelled blood, and he thought he was coming in for the kill.

"Why don't you just tell me what happened? It'll be so much easier," he said, and he again blew smoke into my face.

I could tell him everything that happened for the last two weeks, but it would be a waste of time. Most of what I could tell him could implicate just about anybody, which would still leave me as the most likely suspect since my prints were on the gun.

"Tell me about the boat," he said.

"What boat?"

"The one you used to take Jenny James out on so you could toss her in the water off Venice. Why don't you tell me about that?"

He sucked on his cigarette and his cheeks sank into his cadaverous face. "You and some other guy rents a boat, and . . . Nah, you tell me?"

Inadvertently, he gave me something Kansas had held back. There were a lot of guys in Los Angeles who could've rented a boat, a lot of people who could be working for whoever had been setting me up since my first day on the job. Wells and Cheeves were the most likely suspects, but they weren't the only possibilities, and I doubted they were working alone – they weren't smart enough.

"Well?" Derinzi said.

"These two guys rent a boat," I said, "neither of which is me – Now what?"

"What do you mean 'Now what?' "

"Help me with the story," I said. "I don't know how it goes."

"What are you? A wise guy."

"What else do *you* know?" I said.

"You killed these broads," he said.

"Don't say 'broads' like that. It makes you sound like a cheap hood."

"Hey, who's under arrest here?" Derinzi said.

The door flung open and Kansas rushed in. "Go down and get me a ham sandwich," he said. I knew he was watching through the two-way mirror. Now, Derinzi would watch while Kansas interrogated. A second or two after he closed the door, I waved to Derinzi through the mirror.

"Why you trying to be so cute?" said Kansas.

"You don't really think I did this?"

"Makes no difference what I think. It's what I got for evidence that counts."

"Did somebody say I rented a boat?"

"You tell me," said Kansas.

"You mean it was a guess?"

"No guess," he said. "The guy at the marina identified you with Jenny James."

"From what?"

"The description we gave him. He's ready to pick you out of a lineup."

"Me and who else?"

"We don't know."

"You've got two somebody else's and Jenny James. Not me," I said.

"I think he'll pick you out of a lineup," said Kansas.

He sighed and slumped in the chair against the wall. After he studied his fingers for a while, he looked up. "What was in it for you?" he said.

"That's just the point, isn't it?" I said. "Put all this together and there's no point at all, nothing that makes me the killer."

"Why did you go through all that trouble to make her look like Kitty?" he said. It was more an accusation than a question, but it didn't make any more sense than the rest of the interrogation.

I opened my mouth, and for just a second, I was going to tell him about Wells and Cheeves, but I wasn't ready to drop their names on him yet.

"Maybe they wanted to get me off the Noni Light murder," I said, and he lit up his cigar. *Here comes the smoke again*, I thought, and cigar smoke was ugly.

"I saw those pictures of Kitty you had in your apartment," he said.

I was right – a stream of ugly cigar smoke came straight

into my face. It didn't make me want a cigarette; it made me want to throw up.

"I saw the note too," Kansas said. "Somebody did threaten you?"

"If you think somebody threatened me, why do you have me here?" I said.

"Because it's pretty phony handwriting. Anybody could've done it: Kitty, you, anybody."

"You arresting her as an accomplice?"

"Look, Kane. I've taken about as much crap as I'm going to take from you."

He wasn't my friend now. He was a cop doing his job, and he was a good enough cop to keep me from knowing what he was thinking.

"Are you going to book me?"

His face turned crimson.

"Look, Kansas. You and Derinzi are telling me a whole bunch of stuff, but all you've got is some things you found in my apartment. Things I told —" I caught myself, realizing that Derinzi was on the other side of the mirror, and I might be implicating Kansas in the suppression of evidence. Maybe he wasn't my friend at this moment, but I was still his, and I wanted to remain his friend after this whole thing was over. ". . . I told Derinzi how the prints got there."

His back was to the two-way mirror, and he nodded a "Thank you."

"What did you tell him," he said for the benefit of Derinzi and whoever else was on the other side of the mirror.

I went over it again. He expressed the same doubts Derinzi had thrown at me.

"Book me, let me go, or let me get a lawyer," I said.

He walked over to the mirror. Then he turned toward me. "Why'd you do it?"

I shook my head in disgust.

"We got enough evidence to . . ."

"Circumstantial evidence."

". . . enough evidence to put you away for a long time," he said, turning away from the mirror.

"You've hardly got enough evidence to take me to trial," I said. "How about if you let me get a lawyer?"

Kansas sighed and shook his head. "Do you know how guilty you sound?" he said.

"And do you know how stupid this whole thing sounds? Look, Kansas, I didn't kill any of them. You're the one who took me down to the beach, remember?"

"Who was working with you?"

"Kansas . . ." I let his name trail off and I sighed.

He looked at me for a while. Then he shook his head and went into the room where Derinzi was watching us. When he came back, he had a pair of canvas deck shoes in his hand.

It was the pair I brought home from Charlotte Randolph's after I got wet saving her daughter.

"You ever see these?"

"They're mine or a pair a lot like mine," I said.

"What do you own them for?"

"Gumshoe work, I've been watching Lester Randolph on his boat."

"Boat, huh?"

"Boat," I said.

He took a long inhale on his cigar, and I knew it was coming again. Smoke, straight into my face. Not even a pretense that it was an accident. After the smoke cleared, I looked at him, disgusted. I believed even now that he was my friend. Maybe he was just trying to prove something to Derinzi. It was the only thing that made any sense.

The door opened and Derinzi stepped in. "They got that

guy from the marina," he said.

"Which marina," I said, out of curiosity, but Kansas jerked his head toward me as if I had just stuck my foot in my mouth. In a sense, I did.

"What's that mean?" Kansas said.

I explained about Lester Randolph's marina behind Venice. "The guy there saw me a couple of times. He can identify me but he may get me mixed up with whoever rented the boat."

"Sounds like a confession to me," said Derinzi.

"Let's move it," said Kansas, nudging me toward the door. I didn't know whether he was angry or was just making a show for Derinzi.

The other five men in the lineup were cops, all near my height and weight, who roughly fit my description. The one who knew me shook my hand before we stepped into the lineup.

"How'd you get screwed up in this?" he said.

"I'm always getting screwed up in something."

"That's why I got out of private work," he said.

If you've never been in a police lineup, you're missing a treat. The lights glare as you look through a wire screen that keeps what's on the other side into total darkness. You know there are people there just itching to get somebody sent away. The screen gives them anonymity for a while, but many of them are still eager to pin something on somebody – anybody. If you're in the lineup, you stand against the white background in front of the glaring lights for all the world to know you're exactly six-foot-one. You hear voices, but you can hardly make out the words – unless a cop yells at you to do something.

"Number four. Step forward," Derinzi said.

I was number four, so I did as I was told.

"Now say, 'How much for the big boat?' "

"How much for the big boat," I said, and there was a moment of silence.

"Number two, step forward," Derinzi called.

The cop who knew me did as he was told. He was asked to say the same thing and he did. Derinzi asked both of us to stand in profile and we did that. Derinzi called me again and asked me to say "cash on the barrel head."

Then he called Number Two for the same thing. Pretty soon it got like that "Simon says" game we played as kids. Finally Derinzi told us to file off the platform.

"Number Four, you wait in the detention," Derinzi said.

I waited, and in a few minutes Derinzi and Kansas came into the room, smiling.

"He identified you," Derinzi said.

My stomach flipped, but Derinzi was playing a smart-ass. "He says the guy looked like you only better looking, but he didn't sound anything like you."

"Ballistics checked out the snub-nose we found in your place," Kansas grumbled. "It ain't the one that killed them."

"What?" That surprised even me.

"That's it, pal," said Derinzi. I hated when he called me "pal," because we were anything but.

"Somebody went to a lot of trouble to try to prove I *didn't* do it," I said.

"Somebody by the name of Brian Kane," said Derinzi. "You ain't off the hook yet."

"That's enough," said Kansas.

Derinzi was glaring at me and still trying to look tough. His sneer said that if he didn't get me this time, he'd get me the next time around.

"What about my pictures," I said, looking straight

at Derinzi.

"We're gonna hold on to 'em for a while," said Kansas.

"I'd like them back."

"They still might be evidence," said Kansas.

"Pornography," said Derinzi, sneering. "We could arrest you for possession of pornography, you know."

"That so?" I said.

"That's so," said Derinzi.

"But in the meantime, I can leave?" I said.

"You can leave here, but don't leave town," he said.

"Come on," said Kansas, impatiently. "I'll give you a ride home."

We walked silently to his car.

"Don't worry about Derinzi," he said, when he opened the passenger door for me. "He sees too many movies."

"Did the witness really say the guy was better looking?" I said.

"He sure did," said Kansas, sliding behind the wheel of his unmarked police car.

So the man who hired the boat was better looking than me, I thought. It's not that I'm what you'd call handsome, but there were only three men involved in this case who qualified for that "better looking" title. Two of them, Lester Randolph and Roger Francene, were important movie stars and easily identified by just about anybody. Some women might consider Toby Wentworth good looking, but few men wouldn't agree. That left only Cheeves, and I knew where he lived.

I asked Kansas why they picked on me, and he told me an anonymous caller had dropped information that I had possession of the murder weapon.

"Male or female."

"They couldn't tell," Kansas said.

"Just like the call about Lydia Lane's murder," I said, and

we drove for a long time in silence.

"Sorry about your apartment," he said as he let me out in front of my building.

"Yeah," I said.

He was right. My apartment was ripped apart. The so-called clues were gone, but there was a note on the kitchen table from Kitty that said she was going home.

"I can't stand the mess, and I'm not cleaning it up," she added in a P.S.

I called at her place and she filled me in on what happened.

"Did they accuse you of anything?" I said.

"They said I could be an accessory after the fact if I didn't tell them everything I knew. I said I didn't know a damn thing, and I told them to go fuck themselves."

"That's my girl. Do you feel safe by yourself?"

"No, but I'm not coming over to clean up your place, if that's what you're hinting at. You'd better hire somebody."

"I'll do that in the morning," I said. "How about if I come over there?"

"You know better than that," she said.

"Yeah," I said. I always knew better than that, but it was always worth a try. Her house was her private sanctum, the place where she got away from everything including her call business, but I was hoping she'd let me sleep in a nicely decorated place instead of the mess the cops had made of mine. She was right, I should have known better.

"How about a hotel?" I said.

"I do hotels for a living. Find another whore," she said. Her tone was not very friendly, and I understood. I was even a little embarrassed for suggesting it. Kitty was her own woman. She did the things she did because she wanted to do them, including most of the things she was paid to do. She didn't feel she had to explain herself to me or anyone else.

It was one of the things I liked about her, but it was also one of the things I had a lot of trouble handling.

"I got things to do anyhow," I said.

"Get 'em done," she said, and she hung up. Today, she wasn't very sweet. I guess she didn't like the idea that she'd gotten involved in my case.

As I drove toward Wells and Cheeves' house, I tried to figure out why they would go to all the trouble to plant the wrong gun in my apartment while I was still in it. It would have been so much easier to plant it in my office, and they damn sure knew where that was. They could still have dropped the anonymous tip.

There were other things that didn't make sense. If they were hired killers from Chicago or Kansas City, they would have been out of town after the first murder and certainly after the second. It looked like they were just hanging around to get arrested. Not smart, and not what the mob usually did.

I could go a long way to taking myself off the hook if I just gave Kansas everything I had, but there was too much left to interpretation, and I wanted the killer of the three girls. I didn't like the fact that somebody tried to set me up with Noni's murder and tried to scare me off by making the body look like Kitty. And I damn sure didn't like the fact that they killed Lydia while I was supposed to be protecting her. *That* just wasn't good for business.

I didn't think I had all the information I needed to find the killer or killers, but I was getting close. The key was Carla Mahoney and Kansas didn't even know her name yet. At least I didn't think he knew it. If Wells and Cheeves were working for her, they were just heavies. Either or both of them might be the trigger man but she was the brains.

It was already dark when I drove past Wells and Cheeves' house. There were no lights this time, so I parked my Ford on the next street, put on my suede gloves, and walked quickly across the back yards.

CHAPTER 22

I went to the roll-top desk in the upstairs bedroom and opened it. The surface was now cluttered with open makeup, and the aroma of turpentine pervaded the room. There was a mirror, which was understandable, but there was also a framed glamour photo of the Charlotte Randolph look-alike, and a note on the lavender paper I'd seen so much of in the past few days.

"For all those beautiful young girls," the note said, and it was signed with an elaborate feminine signature. Odd, I thought. It was just one name, one familiar name.

I felt a strange discomfort as I searched through the drawers and again studied the photos that were still there: the three murdered girls, plus Gloria Hastings, Kitty, and some others who were presumably still alive. All the photos were like the ones used to blackmail Lester Randolph: candid or taken on the sly by a photographer who had an artistic attitude – except for the ones of Kitty, which were vicious.

The imposter looked like Charlotte all right, I thought looking at the glamour shot.

As I studied the makeup on the desk, I was uncomfortable without quite knowing why. I quickly flashed the light behind me, but I saw no one, and I went back to exploring the makeup. It was not just lipstick, powder and rouge, but little jars of various colored paints. There were half-a-dozen damp, but clean, artist's brushes – the reason for the turpentine smell, I supposed.

It was like someone was getting ready to paint a portrait or had just done so. Yet, the colors were the flesh colors and pink that might be used to make someone look like Kitty or Charlotte Randolph.

I again had the feeling that someone else was in the room, and I again flashed my penlight.

Again, I saw no one, but I took more time. When the beam crossed the bed a second time, I did a double-take to an ugly blotch of red against the wall. I moved the light slowly to the floor and saw feet with spiked heels barely showing from behind the bed. I stepped across the room for a better angle.

A body in a filmy negligee lay face-down on the beige carpet. The head, turned to the side, lay on a blot of red that was at least a foot in diameter and every bit as ugly as the one on the wall. A wig, blown askew by an exit bullet, had the same color and hairstyle as Charlotte's, and a snub-nose .38 dangled from the well-manicured fingers.

I moved closer and held the light on the face, which lay one cheek on the carpet and one cheek up. Even with gloves, I wouldn't touch the body, wouldn't turn it over. Through the filmy material, I saw the elaborately structured chest girdle, with attached, authentic-looking rubber breasts with silver dollar size aureoles. It was like the image in the photos. The face looked like Charlotte, but it was the family resemblance painted to perfection.

It was Roger Francene, in drag, made up in an elaborate finale for the world to know.

The note on the desk had been signed simply, "Francene."

I thought about the day of Noni Light's funeral, when the limousine sped away with the Charlotte look-alike, while the real Charlotte sat up front in the chapel. I thought again about the photos and about what Toby Wentworth had said about Roger being jealous of the pretty young starlets, and I thought about Lester's habit of taking two women to bed at the same time.

I reached for the phone, but I pulled my fingers back before they ever touched the receiver. It made no sense to contaminate any prints with the smudge of my gloves. I was already in too much trouble with Kansas. If I called him with another discovered body, even one that was an apparent suicide, I'd be interrogated again, and I didn't want that. I had too much to do, and it was time to get the hell out of there.

I drove a few blocks and called Charlotte from a booth on Santa Monica. I was prepared to hang up if Lester answered, but I let the phone ring three times.

"This is Charlotte Randolph, may I help you?" she said, sweetly.

"Mrs. Randolph," I said, matching her formality.

"This is she."

"Is there anyone home?" I said.

"Kane?" she whispered.

"Yeah," I said.

There was a long pause. Then she sighed and continued to whisper, "I showed him the pictures. I already got a lawyer. Lester's got the kids on the boat for the weekend. He's trying to explain it to them."

"Can I come over?"

Another pause and a sigh. "My lawyer says it's not a good idea. Suppose I come to your place?"

"It's a mess over there," I said. "The cops were looking for some gun they thought I had."

"I'd still like to see you," she said. I heard the excitement in her voice and I was excited too.

I thought about the same hotel offer I'd made to Kitty but thought better of it. It would have sounded to her just like it sounded to Kitty. Besides, it smacked of disloyalty.

"About a half hour?" I said.

"Good. I'll be right there," she said, and she hung up.

I held the receiver in my hand for a few seconds before I cradled it. Then I decided I'd better get home and clean up for company.

No case that involves murder is ever clean. In the world of real people, jealousy, divorce, and violence are ugly, but movie people want everything wrapped up like the endings of happy films. The trouble is, it never works out that way. In real-life, Hollywood is every bit as ugly as the rest of the world – the players just wear better-looking clothes.

In ten minutes I was home, doing my best to get my apartment ready for visitors. Only fifteen minutes after I arrived, Charlotte was at my door and the only thing I'd managed to straighten up was the bed. Everything else was still in a shambles.

She stepped inside, wearing a wrap-around poplin trench coat, black gloves and black, high-heeled shoes. She closed the door and leaned her back against it.

"Nice place," she said sarcastically.

"I told you it was a mess."

"It'll do," she said.

For a moment, she stayed against the door, smiling. Then she moved toward me, slipped her arms around my neck and kissed me full and lingering as if we were lovers who hadn't quite lost the newness of romance. In a sense, that was true, but it wasn't real.

"Your brother's dead," I said, sliding away from the kiss.

"What?" Her fingers went limp and slipped from my neck. She stood quietly for a moment, tears glistening. Then she pushed past me and went deeper into my apartment.

"It looks like he killed himself. He left a note. 'For all those beautiful young girls,' it said. He was in drag, and he signed it with just his last name."

"Just 'Francene'?" she said with a wistful smile. "He called himself that when we were kids. That's why he used it on the screen."

"He was painted to look like you," I said.

"He always wanted to look like me. Why didn't you tell me on the phone?"

"I was afraid you wouldn't come over."

"I would have. No I wouldn't, I . . . I don't know."

She looked straight at me. A weak smile turned up at one corner of her mouth, her tears still glistening. She was so tempting, so desirable even in the wake of her brother's death, that I let her step into my arms. She nestled her head against my shoulder and stayed that way for a long time. Then she twisted her head upward.

"I need to be comforted," she said. "Is this is a good time? A good place?"

"Yes," I said. I thought about Kitty, and I felt like a liar – not only to Kitty, but to Charlotte, and maybe even to myself.

She brushed her tears with the knuckle of her velvet glove. Then she crossed to the bedroom, turned and framed herself in the doorway. She undid the sash of her trench coat, and the poplin material rustled open. Except for her garter belt and stockings, she was naked down the middle. She smiled broadly, but there was hurt in her eyes. She peeled the coat from her shoulders and let it slide to the floor. Her velvet gloves went all the way to her elbows.

"Mourning period over so soon?" I said.

She twisted her brow, confused for just a moment. Then she shrugged almost imperceptibly and stepped toward me, spreading her fingers and holding out her arms. If things were different, even my feelings for Kitty wouldn't stand in the way of my making love to her at this moment, but there was more to it.

"Do you always play the circle against the center?" I said.

As if she hadn't heard me, she stepped forward for another kiss, but I held her away.

"Do you think I can't tell a man from a woman?"

"What are you talking about?" she said, trying to kiss me, her breath so very sweet.

"That wasn't your brother who came to hire me. It was you."

She twisted out of my arms, crossed the room and pulled back the curtains. She looked as good from behind as she did from the front, and much better than the so-called extortion photos when she was a few years younger and heavier, and where she had painted or rouged huge moons around her nipples to appear to be a different person. She finally turned toward me, still smiling.

"This is such a good time and such a good place. Let's not ruin it," she said.

"It might have been great, but it's over."

She framed herself as a shadow in the window. She brought the fingers of her left hand to her hip, tilted her head, and thrust her pelvis forward as temptingly as Eve to Adam. She was so beautiful. If I didn't know she was so treacherous, I would have fallen without a thought.

"Do you want me with the stockings on or off?" she said.

"You came to my office three weeks ago just to set me up," I said.

She didn't reply, she just stood there, moving ever so subtly: a bent knee, a crooked elbow, a thrust hip.

"I've never been to your office."

"As the real Charlotte, you never came to my apartment either, but you knew where I lived. I never told you where I live, made it a point not to, but you got here just fine and damn quick too."

"You're crazy," she said, and she pouted. She knew all the weapons of seduction.

"You had it all worked out, but you blew it."

"I don't know what you're talking about?"

"You're brother wasn't a good enough actor to convince me up close that he was a woman, even fully clothed. Then I called you, and you started to speak like a true, Beverly Hills matron. You used charm school diction. You thought you caught yourself in time, but you didn't. It wasn't the first time you fell out of that fake, roughness, it was just the first time I fully realized it."

"You're so silly." She was trying coy, but it was too late.

"You're speaking so beautifully now: clean, California English. Not the slurred words of the woman you think I consider to be the real Charlotte Randolph. If you had thought of it, you would have used the rough accent when you came to me the first time, but you didn't think of it yet. You were disguised perfectly – a little extra padding in the bra, a little extra something at the hips, a lot of paint on the face. You thought that image would match those old photos if I saw them, and, if not, you thought it would match the image of a man in drag."

She twisted her brow, actually trying to make it look as if I had hurt her feelings.

"I don't know what you're saying," she said softly. She took a step toward me again. "You're talking crazy."

"You knew Roger was running around town dressed as you, and you knew about Noni and Lester, but you didn't want anybody to know you even suspected him. That would be very un-Charlotte like. After all, a Hollywood matron who runs her own home, takes care of her own kids? Her marriage could never be questioned: not even by herself when she had her own secret lovers. Someone else would have to spring it on you. That's why you invented the fake Charlotte, the ultra-feminine Charlotte, so overly feminine that in retrospect, I might be convinced you were a man in drag."

Now she tried to look confused.

"I suspected your brother only for a couple of seconds after I found the body, but it was you I really suspected, and when I talked to you on the phone, that was the clincher." Even now, I surveyed her body.

"You *are* crazy," she said, stepping past me toward the bedroom. "No one would try anything that stupid."

"No one, except a woman who thought she was an absolutely brilliant actress. I had to piece everything together. What I don't understand is why the game? Was your whole plan to kill Lester's women? Or to kill your brother? What was it all about?"

"Make love to me Kane," she said, backing into the bedroom and reaching out with both hands, her fingers spread toward me.

"Don't you hear what I'm saying?" I said.

"Sure, I hear, and it makes me want you even more."

She turned both palms just inches under her breasts, threatening to touch them. I felt like I was being seduced by a vampire. I wasn't afraid, but I was mesmerized and curious. What kind of woman was she to want to seduce the man who was about to send her to jail? Or was that just the point?

"Why should you trust me? I killed them all." Even those

words were part of her ploy, and I knew it.

"There's no way you could have killed them by yourself."

"But I did. Don't you see? It was too complicated to get anyone else involved. If too many people knew, it would be too easy to get caught. I set Roger up with Billy and Teddy. If the cops suspect murder instead of suicide, they're the ones who will go to jail."

"Sure. You didn't use them at all," I said.

"You don't believe me?"

"You probably haven't told the truth in years."

She reached out with her gloved hand and touched my cheek. Her scent invade first my nostrils, then my brain. She was getting me closer to a point where there would be no turning back, to a point where I would make love to her and hold her for the cops, or make love to her and live to regret it, yet right now it all seemed worth it.

"It was you, Wells and Teddy Cheeves all the time," I said. "At first, all you wanted to do was get something on Lester, but that changed somewhere along the way, maybe it was after I told you there were more women than just Noni. After that, you wanted to get them all. You didn't get Gloria Hastings because you've got those pictures I took, and you need her testimony. I don't read minds, but I make good guesses."

Her tightly gloved fingers moved from my cheek and down to the top button of my shirt.

"You've been a detective too long, Mr. Kane," she said.

Even her use of the word "Mister" was seductive. She was more beautiful than the young things she killed, and she was far more a woman, far more intelligent. I knew this seduction was part of her plan. Yet, I wanted to be drawn into it and I was willing to take the chance that I could get myself out.

First I had to see how much more information I could get. I pushed her hand away from my collar. "You killed Noni and

Lydia all by yourself, but I think your Keystone crooks rented the boat for you so you could kill Jenny James and dump her body in the water. The sharks getting a couple of chunks out of her was just a bonus. I'm sure you were the makeup artist on that too. You're very good at that."

"You're crazy," she whispered, and in the last few minutes, "crazy" had become an extremely sexy word.

"You set your brother up with Wells and Cheeves in that phony limousine thing. You had him show up at Noni Light's funeral. I'm sure you told him it was just for fun, but the idea was for me to get the tag number and track them to Roger. Since that didn't work, you got them to threaten me and hope I got the tag number a second time. To make it look even more like a threat, you had to kill Jenny James and make her look like Kitty. What I don't understand is how you can be so vicious and yet be such a good mother?"

"That has nothing to do with it," she growled, her eyes going wide. She took one hard step toward me in a rage. Then she stopped and her expression softened. If she hadn't taken control of her role as seductress, she might have torn my eyes out. Instead, she touched my shirt again, and slowly undid the buttons.

"You're good with these things," I said.

"You don't really understand women, do you?"

"What man does? . . . Why did you kill your brother?"

"Shut up," she said, and she went back to the silencing kiss.

My hands slid over her back, gripped her buttocks, and pulled her hard against me. Her lips slid away, and her mouth fell open in a rasping intake of breath.

"Why did you kill your brother? You had me all set up to take the fall. My prints on the gun –"

"Shut up," she whispered, and she clicked her teeth against mine and sucked my breath through her parted lips.

"Because you hated him? Because he became the star and you didn't?"

"Yes, you bastard. Yes, that was it," she said, and she slapped me hard across the cheek.

"You're beautiful," I said, but knowing I was in the presence of a killer, I crossed to the night table, picked up the phone, and jiggled the cradle for the operator.

"Who are you calling?" Charlotte said.

"The police," I said, jiggling again.

"Put it down," someone said. It was a male voice.

I glanced at the doorway, surprised to see Teddy Cheeves, standing behind Charlotte with a .38 snub in his hand. Charlotte was smiling, totally satisfied with her performance. I saw no point in arguing, so I lowered the receiver to the night table.

"Why did you get naked?" Cheeves said, looking straight into her eyes.

"I gave you the signal at the window. If you didn't want me to do anything, you should have gotten here sooner."

She picked up her poplin trench coat, slipped into it, and knotted the belt.

"You're dumb for a detective," she snarled, as she snatched the snub-nose .38 from Cheeves.

She was right. Sometimes, I let the wrong organ do my thinking, but I hoped that in other regards I had done the right thing.

"You were right about my brother," she said. "That son of a bitch got to be a star. And all I got to be was Lester's housekeeper."

Without changing the inflection of her voice, she swung the snub-nose in Teddy's direction and fired one shot right into the middle of his chest.

He stumbled backwards out of the room, and I started

after her, but before I took half-a-step, she swung the gun back at me.

I wanted to grab it, but she didn't hold it nearly so loosely as when she wanted me to take if from her. If I went after it, I might get one in the chest too, so I thought better of it.

"Now you," she said, snarling.

"How do you think you'll get away with this? You've killed half the god damned people in Hollywood."

"No, You and Roger and Teddy and Billy killed half the people in Hollywood. You left a suicide note, just like Roger."

"Sure I did."

"Your note says, 'A man's got to make a living.'"

They were the words she asked me to write, the words that seemed so stupid at the time, the words for her so-called screenplay.

"It's not much of a suicide note," I said.

"Neither is 'All those beautiful young girls,' but it will do. You know, Kane, I always wear gloves when . . ." She smiled. "When I pull the trigger. Good bye, Kane. Can I have a profile?"

"Nope."

She moved closer. "Then I'll shoot you in the face."

I started to back across the room toward the night table. "A lot of suicides blow away their own face, but without powder burns, you're going to have a hard time convincing anybody it was suicide."

"Don't play with me, Kane," she said. She raised the gun, stepped closer, and took a straight aim at my face. I stared the short length of the barrel to her sighting eye as she moved even closer, with her arm outstretched.

"Open your mouth," she said.

"You *are* nuts," I said.

The barrel was pointing at my nose now, and she was about to take another step, which would have been plenty close enough for powder burns, maybe even enough to convince a police lab I pulled the trigger myself.

I'm sure that at the last moment of life, a lot of people realize they're going to die, and I'll bet that many who have been shot saw that twist of the killer's brow as she decided to pull the trigger. I saw that twist of Charlotte's brow, but I'd be damned if I was going to let her kill me.

I swung my head to the right and batted the gun to the left. The snub-nose went off like a cannon. The slug whizzed past my left ear and the blast burned my face. She swung the muzzle back in my direction and fired again, but she overcompensated and the slug slashed through my right arm, tearing a chunk out of it. My right arm hurt like hell but I grabbed for the gun with my left hand and caught her wrist.

She came up with a very unladylike knee to my groin but I wasn't about to get killed over the pain. In the tight quarters of my bedroom, I held onto her wrist and she fired again. This time the shot went wild and chunked into the ceiling. With her left hand, she grabbed my crotch and held on. I struggled to get the gun away from her and she growled like a tigress. She tried to turn the gun at a downward angle. Now, instead of pointing at me, it was pointed at the wall behind my head and the angle was closing toward my face.

I didn't know how much blood I had lost but the whole right side of my body was wet. If I lost too much, I would pass out and that would be it. She'd have me. I'd be dead, but she'd never get away with my murder – note or no note. It was the kind of stupid thinking you get as you go into shock. Her not getting away with murder would be no consolation if I were dead.

I dropped my feet out from under me and fell to my knees and she lost her grip on my groin, but the angle of the gun came downward and she fired again. This time, the slug took a chunk out of the night table behind me, but the pain in my groin subsided, and I bent her wrist hard. The gun thumped to the floor and she dove after it.

I thought I heard a police siren, but time was short and I could count on nothing. I caught her coat and climbed up her back. I grabbed her right arm with my left hand and pulled it back, but I was losing a lot of blood. She snapped back with her head, trying to crack my nose with her skull, but my face was to the side and she caught me on the cheek. The blood from my arm poured over Persian carpet.

"You son of a bitch!" she cried.

"Yeah," I said, but I held onto her. I tried to regain control of everything, but I was losing too much blood and I was getting light-headed. I started to think about sharks again. She must have realized something was happening and she continued the steady pressure of reaching for the gun and now she was trying to reach with her left hand.

I saw the .38 on the floor, and I might even be able to release her and grab it, but I couldn't take the chance. It was a waiting game now, and if she out-waited me, I was dead.

The police siren was loud and sharks were swimming in circles, I thought. I started to imagine other things. I was still holding her on the floor but she was standing over me too, and that didn't make sense, especially when she stooped and picked up the gun.

No, I thought, and I looked up at her, but it wasn't Charlotte.

"Kitty?" I said, confused.

"Kansas is on the way up," she said.

"What are you doing here?"

"I came to straighten out your apartment," she said.

"Huh?" I said. I didn't know what she was talking about.

I released Charlotte and sat back on my haunches,

wavering. Kitty held the gun and Charlotte didn't move. I was next to the table and I saw the phone off the hook, and I remembered what I had done.

Even during the struggle, it just lay on the table with the open line to the telephone company.

In a daze, I picked up the receiver and spoke into the mouthpiece. "Hello?" I said.

"That was so exciting," said the operator. "Just like in the movies."

"Yeah, just like in the movies."

"I called the police for you."

"Thanks," I said, and Kansas rushed into the room along with his pal, Derinzi.

"He tried to kill me!" Charlotte shouted.

"Sure he did, Lady," said Kansas, and that was the last I remembered for a while.

When I regained consciousness, I was in a hospital with my right arm in a cast. Kitty was sleeping in the chair next to my bed.

"No fares tonight?" I said, my voice weak.

She opened her eyes and smiled, but the smile suddenly disappeared, and she said, "What were you doing with her?"

"Trying to keep from getting killed."

"Sure you were."

"Did they find Roger Francene?"

"And some guy named Wells. Kansas still wants to know how you figure it, because he can't – except for what that telephone operator tells him, and all she does is confuse him." Kitty chuckled. "Andrea Anderson is calling Charlotte Randolph 'The Dragon Lady.'"

"That's what she calls every woman who's ever killed more than one person," I said.

"I've noticed that."

"What about her kids?"

"Her kids? Oh, Lester has 'em."

"At least they've got somebody," I said.

Charlotte's children losing their mother was just another sad part of the whole thing, but they'd survive. A lot of kids had survived worse.

"Yeah. It's nice to have somebody, even if you have to share a little."

She smiled and squeezed my hand, and her tears glistened.

We had each other. It was weird, but it was nice weird, and we weren't sure what we were to each other. The word "friends" was too weak. "Lovers" wasn't right either.

What we had, we couldn't give a name, but I was damn glad we had it.

The best in all-new neo-noir, hard-boiled and retro-pulp mystery and crime fiction.

Autumn 2001 Release

FLESH AND BLOOD SO CHEAP

A Joe Hannibal Mystery

Wayne D. Dundee

The popular St. Martins hardcover and Dell paperback series is revived! Hard-boiled Rockford, Illinois P.I. Joe Hannibal is at it again, this time swept up in a murderous mystery in a Wisconsin summer resort town. Deception and death lurk behind the town's idyllic façade, when a grisly murder is discovered and Hannibal knows for a fact that the confessed killer couldn't have done the deed!

It'll take two fists and a lot of guts to navigate through the tacky tourist traps, gambling dens and gin mills to get to the truth, while dangerous dames seem determined to steer Hannibal clear of the town's darkest secrets. In the end, Hannibal himself, and everyone he cares for, may be in jeopardy as he learns that murder may be the smallest crime of all in this lakeside getaway!

> *"Mike Hammer is alive and well and operating out of Rockford, Illinois."*
> **Andrew Vachs**

1-891946-16-1   Trade pb, 272 pages

Winter 2001 Release

WAITING FOR THE 400

A Northwoods Noir

Kyle Marffin

They found the first girl in the Chicago train station, a dime-a dance and a quarter-for-more chippy. Suicide. A train ticket still clutched in her hand: Watersmeet Michigan, the end of line…

400 miles north, Watersmeet station master Jess Burton wastes away in his tiny northwoods depot with big dreams big city life, watching the high-rollers and their glamour gals hop off the train for their lakeside mansions and highbrow resorts. Till the night Nina appeared on the depot platform.

Nina…Big city beautiful and clearly marked 'property of'. The kind of dame that can turn a man's head, turn him inside out and upside down till danger doesn't matter anymore, till desire can only lead to death. Because folks *are* dying now, and Jess is in over his head, waiting for the 400 and the red-headed beauty to step off the train with his ticket out of town.

1-891946-14-5   Trade pb, 288 pages

Now try the finest in traditional supernatural horror!

Summer 2001 Release

...DOOMED TO REPEAT IT

D.G.K. Goldberg

It's a miracle that sassy, self-proclaimed punk-cowgirl Layla MacDonald hasn't gone off the deep end: Her mother gruesomely murdered in one of Charlotte, North Carolina's most scandalous love triangles, 'Daddy-Useless' drinking himself into despair, another temp job leading nowhere fast, and the painful memories of her boyfriend's abuse still as fresh as open wounds. Till she meets Ian. And suddenly, dormant desires are awakened. Madness is unleashed. Surreal violence explodes.

Because Ian is a ghost...

...The wandering ghost of an 18th century Scottish rebel, compelled by dark forces neither he nor Layla understand, seeking vengeance for 300 year-old horrors from the bloody highland battlefields. Their fates are bound together, and Ian is driven to protect Layla, with violent consequences, as madness and lust simmer amidst the ethereal world of lost spirits. Now under suspicion for Ian's rampages, the law's on Layla's tail, and her only escape may be to join her spirit lover, both of them doomed to repeat an endless cycle of ghostly horrors.

1-891946-12-9   Trade pb, 272 pages

Autumn 2001 Release

NIGHT PLAYERS

P.D.Cacek

Welcome to Las Vegas, home to glittering casinos, to high stakes, high-rollers, high priced call girls. 'Round the clock vice, where the nightlife never ends. It's the perfect place for a new-born vampire to make her home.

Meet Allison Garret, the unluckiest gal who ever became a vampire, with an irreverently sharp tongue to go along with her sharp teeth. Meet her sidekick, Mica, a Bible-thumping street corner preacher. Both of them are on the run from the catty coven of L.A. strip-club vampire vixens they narrowly escaped from in P.D. Cacek's Stoker Award nominated debut novel *Night Prayers*. Hiding out in Las Vegas, Allison's now a night-shift showgirl, while Mica tries in vain to bring the good book to gamblers, crooks and hookers. And everything's as idyllic as it can be for a preacher and a vampire setting up house in sin city. Till the evil vampire that cruelly turned Allison shows up along with his bloodthirsty minions, and it'll take more than a gambler's luck to save Allison and Mica this time!

1-891946-11-0   Trade pb, 256 pages

Autumn 2001 Release

MARTYRS

Edo van Belkom

250 years ago, French Jesuits erected a mission deep in the uncharted Canadian wilderness, till they were brutally murdered by a band of Mohawks. Or so the legends say.

Today St. Clair College stands near the legendary massacre site, the mission's memory now more folklore than fact. Then St. Clair professor Father Karl Desbiens and his band of eager grad students set off to locate the mission ruins. The site's discovered, artifacts are found, the mystery of the Mohawk massacre may be solved…

…Till the archeological dig accidentally unearths an old world evil. There was no 'Mohawk massacre'. A malevolent demonic power was imprisoned in the remote Canadian wilderness by the original missionaries. But now it's been unleashed. Now the nightmare will commence. Father Desbiens has his own inner demons to struggle with, his own crisis of faith to overcome. He's an unlikely martyr to the faith he already questions, but the demonic presence has invaded St. Clair college, leaving a bloody trail of horror among his students.

1-891946-13-7   Trade pb, 272 pages

The Horror Writers Association

BELL, BOOK & BEYOND

An Anthology Of Witchy Tales

Edited by P.D. Cacek

Stoker Award winner P.D. Cacek brings you 21 bewitching stories about wiccans, warlocks and witches, all written by the newest voices in terror: the Affiliate Members of the Horror Writers Association. From fearsome and frightening to starkly sensual and darkly humorous, each tale will cast its own sorcerous spell, leaving you anxiously looking for more from these new talents!

1-891946-19-9   Trade pb, 320 pages

A FACE WITHOUT A HEART

A Modern-Day Version Of Oscar Wilde's
The Picture Of Dorian Gray

Rick R. Reed

Nominated for the 2001 Spectrum Award for "Best Novel": A stunning retake on the timeless themes of guilt, forgiveness and despair in Oscar Wilde's fin de siecle classic, *The Picture Of Dorian Gray*. Amidst a gritty background of nihilistic urban decadence, a young man's soul is bargained away to embrace the nightmarish depths of depravity – and cold blooded murder – as his painfully beautiful holographic portrait reflects the ugly horror of each and every sin.

"A rarity: a really well-done update that's as good as its source material."
Thomas Deja, Fangoria Magazine

"A startling study of human nature and of its most potent desires and fears...
Rick Reed is truly one of the best around today."
Sandra DeLuca, Graveline

1-891946-08-0   Trade pb, 256 pages

GOTHIQUE

A Vampire Novel

Kyle Marffin

International Horror Guild Award nominee Kyle Marffin takes you on a tour of the dark side of the darkwave, when a city embraces the grand opening of a new 'nightclub extraordinaire', Gothique, mecca for the disaffected Goth kids and decadent scene-makers. But a darker secret lurks behind its blacked-out doors and the true horror of the undead reaches out to ensnare the soul of a city in a nightmare of bloodshed, and something much worse than death.

"An awfully good writer...this is a novel with wit and edge, engaging characters and sleazy ones for balance, a keen sense of melodramatic movement and a few nasty chills."
Ed Bryant, Locus Magazine

"Bloody brilliant! A white-knuckle adventure filled with plenty of chills and thrills...this book just never lets up."
M. McCarty, The IF Bookworm

1-891946-06-4   Trade pb, 448 pages

WHISPERED FROM THE GRAVE

An Anthology Of Ghostly Tales

Quietly echoing in a cold graveyard's breeze, the moaning wails of the dead, whispered from the grave to mortal ears with tales of desires unfulfilled, of dark vengeance, of sorrow and forgiveness and love beyond the grave. Includes tales by Edo van Belkom, Tippi Blevins, Sue Burke, P.D. Cacek, Dominick Cancilla, Margaret L. Carter, Don D'Ammassa, D.G.K. Goldberg, Barry Hoffman, Tina Jens, Nancy Kilpatrick, Kyle Marffin, Julie Anne Parks, Rick R. Reed and David Silva.

"A chilling collection of ghost stories...each with a unique approach to ghosts, spirits, spectres and other worldly apparitions...Pleasant nightmares."
Michael McCarty, Indigenous Fiction

1-891946-07-2   Trade pb, 256 pages

STORYTELLERS

Julie Anne Parks

A writer who once ruled the bestseller list with novels of calculating horror flees to the backwoods of North Carolina. A woman desperately fights to salvage a loveless marriage. A storyteller emerges — the keeper of the legends — to ignite passions in a dormant heart. But an ancient evil lurks in the dark woods, a malevolent spirit from a storyteller's darkest tale, possessing one weaver of tales and threatening another in a sinister and bloody battle for a desperate woman's life and for everyone's soul.

"A macabre novel of supernatural terror, a book to be read with the lights on and the radio playing!"
Bookwatch

"A page-turner, for sure, and a remarkable debut."
Triad Style

"Genuine horror and the beauty of the Carolina wilds. It's an intoxicating blend."
Lisa DuMond, SF Site

1-891946-04-8   Trade pb, 256 pages

THE DARKEST THIRST

A Vampire Anthology

Sixteen disturbing tales of the undead's darkest thirsts for power, redemption, lust...and blood. Includes stories by Michael Arruda, Sue Burke, Edo van Belkom, Margaret L. Carter, Stirling Davenport, Robert Devereaux, D.G.K. Goldberg, Scott Goudsward, Barb Hendee, Kyle Marffin, Deborah Markus, Paul McMahon, Julie Anne Parks, Rick R. Reed, Thomas J. Strauch, and William Trotter.

"Fans of vampire stories will relish this collection."
Bookwatch

"If solid, straight ahead vampire fiction is what you like to read, then The Darkest Thirst is your prescription."
Ed Bryant, Locus Magazine

"Definitely seek out this book."
Mehitobel Wilson, Carpe Noctem Magazine

1-891946-00-5   Trade pb, 256 pages

SHADOW OF THE BEAST

Margaret L. Carter

Carter has thrilled fans of classic horror for nearly thirty years with anthologies, scholarly non-fiction and her own long running small press magazine. Here's her exciting novel debut, in which a nightmare legacy arises from a young woman's past. A vicious werewolf rampages through the dark streets of Annapolis, and the only way she can combat the monster is to surrender to the dark, violent power surging within herself. Everyone she loves is in mortal danger, her own humanity is at stake, and much more than death may await her under the shadow of the beast.

> *"Suspenseful, well crafted adventures in the supernatural."*
> **Don D'Ammassa, Science Fiction Chronicle**

> *"Tightly written...a lot of fun to read. Recommended."*
> **Merrimack Books**

> *"A short, tightly-woven novel...a lot of fun to read...recommended."*
> **Wayne Edwards, Cemetary Dance Magazine**

1-891946-03-X   Trade pb, 256 pages

NIGHT PRAYERS

P.D. Cacek

Nominated for the prestigious Horror Writers Association Stoker Award for First Novel. A wryly witty romp introduces perpetually unlucky thirtysomething Allison, who wakes up in a seedy motel room — as vampire without a clue about how to survive! Now reluctantly teamed up with a Bible-thumping streetcorner preacher, Allison must combat a catty coven of strip club vampire vixens, in a rollicking tour of the seamy underbelly of Los Angeles.

> *"Further proof that Cacek is certainly one of horror's most important up-and-comers."*
> **Matt Schwartz**

> *"A gorgeous confection, a blood pudding whipped to a tasty froth."*
> **Ed Bryant, Locus Magazine**

> *"A wild ride into the seamy world of the undead... a perfect mix of helter-skelter horror and humor."*
> **Michael McCarty, Dark Regions/Horror Magazine**

1-891946-01-3   Trade pb, 224 pages

THE KISS OF DEATH
An Anthology Of Vampire Stories

Sixteen writers invite you to welcome their own dark embrace with these tales of the undead, both frightening and funny, provocative and disturbing, each it's own delightfully dangerous kiss of death. Includes stories by Sandra Black, Tippi Blevins, Dominick Cancilla, Margaret L. Carter, Sukie de la Croix, Don D'Ammassa, Mia Fields, D.G.K. Goldberg, Barb Hendee, C.W. Johnson, Lynda Licina, Kyle Marffin, Deborah Markus, Christine DeLong Miller, Rick R. Reed and Kiel Stuart.

"Whether you're looking for horror, romance or just something that will stretch your notion of 'vampire' a little bit, you can probably find it here."
Cathy Krusberg, The Vampire's Crypt

"Readable and entertaining."
Hank Wagner, Hellnotes

"The best stories add something to the literature, whether actually pushing the envelope or at least doing what all good fiction does, touching the reader's soul."
Ed Bryant, Locus

1-891946-05-6   Trade pb, 304 pages

CARMILLA: THE RETURN
Kyle Marffin

Marffin's provocative debut — nominated for a 1998 International Horror Guild Award for First Novel — is a modern day retelling of J. S. LeFanu's classic novella, Carmilla. Gothic literature's most notorious female vampire, the seductive Countess Carmilla Karnstein, stalks an unsuspecting victim through the glittery streets of Chicago to the desolate northwoods and ultimately back to her haunted Styrian homeland, glimpsing her unwritten history while replaying the events of the original with a contemporary, frightening and erotic flair.

"A superbly written novel that honors a timeless classic and will engage the reader's imagination long after it has been finished."
The Midwest Book Review

"If you think you've read enough vampire books to last a lifetime, think again. This one's got restrained and skillful writing, a complex and believable story, gorgeous scenery, sudden jolts of violence and a thought provoking final sequence that will keep you reading until the sun comes up."
Fiona Webster, Amazon

"Marffin's clearly a talented new writer with a solid grip on the romance of blood and doomed love."
Ed Bryant, Locus Magazine

1-891946-02-1   Trade pb, 304 pages

Look for these other titles from The Design Image Group at your favorite bookstore. Or visit us at **www.designimagegroup.com** for links to your favorite on-line and specialty booksellers.

To order direct, send check or money order for $15.95 per book, payable in U.S. funds to:

The Design Image Group, Inc.
P.O. Box 2325
Darien, Illinois 60561 USA

Please add $2.00 postage & handling for the first book,
$1.00 for each additional book ordered. Please allow 2-3 weeks for delivery.